Charles Warren Stoddard

A Troubled Heart and How It Was Comforted at Last

Charles Warren Stoddard

A Troubled Heart and How it Was Comforted at Last

ISBN/EAN: 9783337266851

Printed in Europe, USA, Canada, Australia, Japan

Cover: Foto ©Andreas Hilbeck / pixelio.de

More available books at **www.hansebooks.com**

A TROUBLED HEART

AND

HOW IT WAS COMFORTED
AT LAST

BY

CHARLES WARREN STODDARD

NOTRE DAME, INDIANA:
THE AVE MARIA.

TO

THE REV. DANIEL E. HUDSON, C. S. C.,

THIS

AUTOBIOGRAPHY IS LOVINGLY

INSCRIBED.

Let it amaze no one that I have at last chosen to unveil my heart to the possibly unsympathetic eye of the general reader.

Again and again, and yet again, I have been curiously questioned by those who could not follow in the path which led me away from my kinsmen and my comrades, and to whom the mysterious influences which I found irresistible were unknown, or with whom they were of no avail.

What my lips dared scarcely utter—for the decorous recital of an experience so precious to me demanded fit audience and a seasonable hour—my pen in the serene solitude of my chamber has related unreservedly through the pages of THE AVE MARIA. O blessed task accomplished! I have set my lamp, though feeble be its flame, where perchance it may light the feet of some bewildered pilgrim. I have cast my bread upon the waters, hopefully awaiting the return— after many days.

NOTRE DAME, INDIANA,
Feast of the Purification, 1885.

Fool, said the spirit unto me, look into thy
heart and write.
SIR PHILIP SIDNEY.

The heart hath its tears.
FATHER FABER.

A TROUBLED HEART AND HOW IT WAS COMFORTED AT LAST.

I.

I was a lonely child. Blessed with brothers and a sister near my own age; nourished always in the tenderest paternal and maternal love; surrounded by troops of friends, whose affection was won without effort, and whose sympathy was shown in a thousand pretty, childish ways, I was still lonely, and often loneliest when least alone.

It was my custom, when my heart was light and my spirit gay, to steal apart from my companions, and, throwing myself upon the lawn, look upon them in their sports as from a dim distance. Their joy was to me like a song, to which I listened with a kind of rapture, but in which I seldom or never joined. Love, intense and absorbing love, and love alone, was my consolation. This love I know, and have always known; but love has its antipode: it is not hate, but fear.

Very early in life I learned to know fear. I was afraid of strange faces, and more than all else I was afraid of the dark. How often, when alone in my room at night, have I buried my face in my pillow, to shut out the visions I saw not, yet feared that I might see! When the light was extinguished, I seemed suddenly translated to some unknown world, which my imagination peopled vaguely; and the approach of these invisible and shapeless forms was what I dreaded. Alas! how many innocent little ones are now suffering as I was wont to suffer in the solitude of the night, when a single syllable of love might dispel the direst chimeras!

The God to whom I had been carefully taught to pray, whose majesty and glory were beyond my comprehension; whose image was not before me; whose nature came not within the range of my conception,—that God seemed never to have set one star of hope within the blackness of darkness that flooded the fearful night of my infancy. It was not the love of God that filled my heart then, but rather the fear of Him who I had been taught was a jealous God, visiting His wrath upon the sinful: and were we not all sinners? No voice spoke to me out of that fathomless gloom; I drifted on and on, among formless shades, tremblingly awaiting the return of day.

.　.　.　.　.　.

Our old home in the city stood upon a street corner, opposite a Gothic church built of rough

gray stone. Every morning this
church was thronged, and on
Sundays it seemed to me that
services would never end there.
This amazed me; for we children
were taken to a church on Sunday only—a day which was
called "Sabbath" among my
people,—and when the eleven
o'clock sermon was ended, and
the "Sabbath school," which
followed it, was over, we
returned home, and remained
there, being too young to be
taken out to the evening sermon
or lecture.

Many a time did I listen to
the music that was wafted from
that beautiful church over the
way. It was music unlike any
that I had ever heard,—music
that soothed and comforted me,
yet at the same time filled me
with an indefinable yearning.
At evening, when the light
streamed through the richly-
tinted windows; when beyond
the doors that swung to and

fro I caught glimpses of clustering tapers, twinkling like dim
stars through clouds of vapor;
when I heard thrilling voices
soaring in ecstasy above the
solemn swell of the organ,— it
seemed to me that heaven must
be in there; the heaven which
my mind refused to picture, and
the thought of which, until now,
had been embittered by the cruel
shadow of death. Once, and
once only, did I enter this chapel
—my little heaven on earth. I
went thither with our maid. I
had begged her to take me;
and, without leave, we went
together. We were early: the
lights burned dimly in the
gathering twilight. I saw for
the first time in my life a
picturesque interior: tapering
columns, pointed arches, rose-
windows, pictures, statues, and
frescoes. I saw an altar that
inspired me with curious awe;
a throng of worshipers, who
knelt humbly and prayed in-

cessantly, so that the quiet of
the chapel was broken by the
soft murmur of lisping lips.
Some one in a long dark robe
came from a hidden chamber
and lighted the candles upon
the altar. This figure seemed of
an unnatural height, and more
slender than any human being
I had ever known; the dark
robe clung weirdly in long,
straight folds; a strange cover-
ing was on the head; it was
the beretta. Where had I seen
something like this before? I
grew pale as I tried to recall a
race of beings clad in these garments, and of whose history I
had somehow gained a knowledge. Then a priest in cope,
attended by a long train of
acolytes, approached the altar.
A faintness and horror seized
me; and, while the hearts of
the worshipers joined the rapt-
urous *Alleluia* of the choir, I
was borne from the chapel in
a paroxysm of terror.

Now I knew, or thought I knew, who these mysterious beings were; I had seen them day after day passing to and fro in a grove overshadowing one wall of the chapel. These, then, were the dark-robed beings who, book in hand, sat or walked in the priests' garden, and whose nature in their passage between the priests' house and the sanctuary had never been clearly revealed to me; indeed, they seemed more shadowy than real as I saw them, over the hedges, flitting in the sombre twilight of the grove. They were such as I had seen again and again as I turned with fluttering heart the leaves of a volume in our library—a chosen volume of Sabbath reading, since it was profusely illustrated with full-page engravings. All that it is possible to devise in the shape of human torture was depicted in this extraordinary book with a boldness that was hardly short of brutality. I returned to it with fearful interest, fascinated by its horrors; it added a new agony to night's dark and wakeful hours. And now, for the first time, I was persuaded that the book was truth, and not a hideous fable! From that hour for long afterward I could not be prevailed upon to occupy my chamber alone, and often it was necessary to leave the lamp lighted until I had fallen asleep.

That book was a Protestant version of the Spanish Inquisition.

II.

The fear I had of the dark-robed priests whom I saw daily moving about in the shadow of the chapel, over the way, grew apace. I solemnly believed that if I were to wander upon the other side of the street, alone and unprotected, one of those grave figures would suddenly pounce upon me, bear me away into the gloom of the grove, and the world would never again see me, or know aught of the tortures to which I had been duly subjected. Nor did this conviction make me any the happier during the long hours I spent in the Protestant church, whither I was invariably taken on the "Sabbath" day.

The meeting house was a large, plastered building, very simple in design, and of the homeliest

description within. There was
a stiff, high pulpit, with a red
cushion upon it, and faded red
draperies behind the sofa, upon
which the minister sat during
the singing of the hymns. The
pews were upholstered in red or
green or brown, according to
the taste of the different owners;
but all else within the building
was of the dullest gray; even
the ungainly windows (which
might have been tinted, for the
sake of the agreeable light they
would then have given) were
painted white, and a thick coat-
ing of dust upon the exterior
made this a dirty gray. There
was nothing in all that dreary
building for the eye to fall on
with a sense of rest; nothing to
· soothe or comfort the heart;
nothing to touch the soul, or to
lift it even for a moment above
the commonplaces of life.

From the moment the preacher
rose in his pulpit to "give out"
the hymns — hymns which were

not pleasing to the ear, and
when drawled by a congregation of indifferent and unculti-
vated voices became anything
but edifying,—I began to long
for the moment when we might
all get out of the place again
into the open air. The minister
stood with his eyes shut and his
hands spread out, while he made
very long, wandering prayers,
at the close of which everybody
bustled and stirred with an
audible sense of relief. When his
sermon was well begun, the
congregation settled into easy
postures, and the monotonous
droning of his voice soon had
visible effect upon some of us.
Heads began to nod in various
parts of the house; and it was
with a kind of fascination that
I watched the bald pate of an
old gentleman, who sat in front
of us, as it lolled upon his shoulders, and was suddenly jerked
up again at intervals, while the
owner of it turned angrily from

right to left, with an expression
of mingled shame and defiance.
I never comprehended any-
thing the minister said. The
monotonous two hours that
comprised the sum and substance of that worship seemed
an eternity to me; I dreaded
it in anticipation, and was
dragged through it Sunday after
Sunday in dumb misery. Sometimes, when a window was
drawn down from the top, a
sunbeam, shattered upon the
waters of a canal that flowed
under one wall of the building,
was reflected upon the ceiling
overhead, where it danced like
a bevy of golden butterflies;
and I was innocently happy in
watching the airy gambols of
those phantom moths. But not
every "Sabbath" was I so fortu-
nate. It was a happy day for
me when, twisting and turning
my neck in childish curiosity, I
discovered a picture upon the
screen beyond which the organ-

blower was secreted; it was an outline of an angel,—an angel. floating through the air with a lute poised lightly upon his breast. Here was something for me to dream over—something to help me to forget for the time being the weariness of the "Sabbath" infliction I was destined to endure: sickness alone being a valid excuse for our stopping away from the "house of worship,"—the sickness which, I fear, we often longed for. My angel in the organ-loft consoled me for a little time only; some one in the pew behind me had noted my wicked fondness for turning my back upon the minister. One day, in the midst of my reverie, when my heart was in the skies with that celestial messenger, the man in the pew behind me seized me abruptly by the shoulders and turned me face about. I was startled and abashed; I feared to look again upon the one object in that

dismal house that could lead my
thoughts to heaven. My last
resource was my father's watch.
With my head nestled upon his
arm, and his watch ticking
softly in my ear, I soon fell
asleep; and if I awoke to find
that the minister was silenced,
and the congregation preparing
for the general visitation which
took place at the close of each
service, I was grateful for the
deliverance that left me free of
a repetition of this mild torture
for seven whole days.

III.

When I was about ten years of
age, we children were taken by
our mother into a far country,
whither our father had preceded
us. Our life there was exciting
and romantic; for we were upon
the frontier, in a new land,
among gold-seekers and advent-
urers; and the children, who
were then few in number, were
made much of. Two years later
it was my lot, and my choice
also, to be sent upon a long sea-
voyage, as companion to an
older brother, who was an in-
valid, in search of health. For
three months we were tossed
upon the waves without setting
foot on shore. Our ship was a
fine one, certainly; but the cap-
tain's wife was the only woman
on board, and there was but
one other passenger beside my

brother and myself. I had not yet acquired a taste for reading; I soon grew weary of playing with the toy-ships the sailors made for me; land we saw only for a few days—not more than five out of the ninety odd,—and it was seldom that our eyes were gladdened by the glimmer of a distant sail. It was a sad experience for me; and my brother, whose health was little benefited, was scarcely able to keep me from yielding to despair.

On leaving home, my mother's last injunction was to read daily some chapters of my Bible, and this I never failed to do. What solemn hours were mine, alone in my cramped state-room, poring over that wonderful volume, and every day becoming more and more perplexed with its histories and mysteries! I did not then know that the wisest heads have disputed over it; that while it is the fountain of all love, it has likewise

watered the seeds of all dis-
sension. It is reasonable to
suppose that the most vigorous
exercise of my private judgment
was not likely to aid me in the
interpretation of even the sim-
plest text. My mental horizon
seemed to grow more and more
limited as I advanced; I was
swallowed up in a solitude as
vast as the sea, and seemed to
be drifting upon a shoreless
waste of waters—alone, helpless,
hopeless.

Again and again I wept in my
perplexity. There was nothing
for me to cling to, not even a
straw; no light shone dimly
upon my pathway; no voice
comforted me in the awful silence
of that weary voyage; and
when, at night, I had kissed my
brother as he lay upon his
painful pillow, and had climbed
into my berth, I heard the hiss
of rushing waters under the keel
of the ship; and, thinking of the
thousand dangers that beset the

mariner upon the trackless sea,
I buried my face in my hands
and trembled in an agony of
suspense.

IV.

At last we came to port and landed safe, three thousand miles from home—twelve thousand by the route we had travelled. For a few weeks I was merry enough; pleased with the novelty of constant change, diverted with much visiting, and likewise with the little local notoriety which my juvenile adventures by land and sea had brought me, I had no care but for the present. The delights of the moment drove from my heart the shadow of a parting that was soon to be.

My brother shortly set forth, alone upon his return voyage, and I was left in charge of my grandfather, who was a thrifty New England farmer. This good man proposed to place me at a neighboring school, of some re-

pute in that part of the country;
there he could visit me at intervals, and it was his hope that
my vacations might be spent
with him. I did not especially
relish the prospect; for though
he loved me dearly, and was not
slow to show it, we were not
much in sympathy. He was a
very honest, practical, much
respected man, of a pronounced
Protestant type: relentless and
even stubborn in his narrow
religious views; he was one in
whose veins the blood had
flowed coldly from the dark
days of the Plymouth Puritans.
Often did I see him nervously
pacing the floor, that shook
beneath his tread, singing with
triumphant voice these lurid
lines:

"On slippery rocks I see them stand,
    While fiery billows roll below."

I know, and I knew even then,
that he believed this to be the
fate of all those whose faith was
not his faith. And yet I never

heard of his having done any one an injury; and when he died a sketch of his life became one of the popular volumes in the "Sabbath-school" libraries.

The new grief in the separation from my brother was gradually wearing away. I liked my school, which was situated about twelve miles from the farm. Once a fortnight my grandfather drove over to see me, and usually brought with him some little gift from the old homestead or from the far-away home. Occasionally I passed a Saturday holiday and Sunday with my grandparents; and stores of baked apples, tarts, and hickory-nuts comforted me in that quiet house.

I was forming new friendships at school,—the fond friendships of boyhood: romantic, chivalrous, noble. We showed one another a kind of devotion worthy of young knighthood, for we were the champions of a wholesome and hearty love. Of course I was subject to periodical attacks of homesickness,—what child away from home is not?—but my new friends rallied in such force, and covered me with such comforting caresses, that my tears, though stormy, were soon dried, and I was a happy boy once more.

Even the long sermons on Sunday seemed to have lost something of their terror for me. Perhaps this was because we boys used to troop into church in a body, and sit in a corner, with our chosen companions next us; no doubt a little spirit of mischief, that was always with us, helped to keep us wide awake till the close of the service.

As the winter vacation drew nigh we were all excitement. A thousand plans were laid and unlaid and relaid, over and over; and it seemed to me that the most joyful season of my life was drawing on. I had been formally invited to spend the holidays with my bosom-friend, in the society of his family, at their elegant home in the city. All the delights of the gay season in the metropolis had been promised us, and the vision of Christmastide was ever before our half-dazzled eyes. It seemed to us that the joyful day of our departure would never, never come.

It never did! In the midst of our enthusiastic preparations for departure, I received from my grandfather an earnest request to abandon the proposed visit and return to him. What could I do? I parted tearfully with my loved companion, and with a heavy heart obeyed.

V.

The snow lay in deep drifts
along the country road; the
fences were often hidden, and
much of the landscape, so beautiful in summer, seemed to have
been effaced forever. Never did
the old farm-house look so deso-
late and forlorn: its windows
half masked in snow, long icicles
hanging from the eaves, and the
brook frozen over and buried
out of sight.

I did not know why I had
been called back to the farm;
but very shortly my grandfather, whose custom it was to
read aloud a chapter in the Bible
night and morning, and follow
the reading with an extempore
prayer, gave me, through the
medium of his prayer, a little
inkling of it.

It seemed that an "Evan-

gelist"—one of those illiterate
enthusiasts who profess special
inspiration from the Almighty—
had fixed upon a neighboring
village as a proper field for his
labors; and there he was daily
and nightly holding meetings of
a sensational character. The
conversions which took place
under his ministrations were
catalogued and advertised far
and wide.

I found my grandparents very
seriously disposed. I hardly
dared to speak. Presently my
grandfather took me aside and
asked me if I did not choose to
love God. Most assuredly I did,
but I had never yet learned how;
for the only God I knew inspired
fear rather than love. Much
was said to me about a "change
of heart," and said in such a
way that I began to feel my
heart must be black indeed and
greatly in need of being changed,
and I the most hardened of
sinners, because the very sight

of the "Evangelist" repelled me, and my soul sickened whenever he or his works were mentioned. My hour of trial had come. I was daily driven three miles through the snow by my grandfather, who would not hear of our missing a single meeting, let it storm or shine. Sometimes we were at the church door before it was open; for promptness was one of the good man's crowning virtues. In these emergencies I remained in the sleigh, while my grandfather hunted up the key of the meeting house, split the wood, and kindled a fire in the huge stove within. Then we sat down in silence and awaited the arrival of the less energetic villagers. Beginning with a chill, that seized me before the fire was lighted, I was driven into a fever through the ill ventilated, over-crowded room, the heat of the red-hot stove, and the unwholesome excitement that prevailed.

There was a bench under the
pulpit which was known as the
"anxious seat"! All those who
were willing to acknowledge
themselves sinners—I remember
that the large majority considered themselves not such;—
all those who desired the
prayers of the prayerful for their
salvation; all those who were
seeking, or desiring, or even
willing to accept that "change
of heart," which was pro-
nounced the one thing needful,
were requested to step forward
in the face of the multitude and
boldly station themselves on
this "anxious seat"—or kneel
by it if they preferred to do so,—
and there undergo the ordeal
of prayer. The spectacle was
humiliating beyond expression.
Nervous excitement and the loss
of all self-control drove the
timid and shamefaced forward
upon this rack of torture. Some
of them, embarrassed and bewildered, wrung their hands and

cried aloud. Once there, they were not permitted to retreat, but, surrounded by half-frantic men and women, whose flushed faces and flashing eyes were fearful to behold, they were held forcibly upon the bench, where they suffered the torments of the damned, until the close of the session.

And I also suffered alike with these. I also was seized by the arm and shaken, because I had stolen into a back seat, stupefied with fear, and knew not when I might go mad like the rest of them. Again I was wickedly shaken, and a wild voice shouted in my ear: "Child, don't you want to be saved?" God knows I did. "Don't you want to be a Christian?" I didn't know what it meant to be a Christian: but I didn't want to be a Christian if the*y* were Christians; so I clenched my hands and clung to my seat, frozen with terror. Then I was dragged from the pew and pushed toward the pulpit, while horrid voices almost shrieked in my ears: "Don't you want to be saved? Do you want to die now, this very minute, and burn forever in hell? Don't you want to be a Christian?" The lie was forced to my trembling lips, and I said "Yes." From that anxious seat I was borne, half senseless, into the open air, and permitted to remain there. Still I heard the shrieks and sobs of the miserable victims within the walls of that bedlam, and all things seemed to swim before my eyes.

It is years since I underwent that degrading inquisition, but to-day I can hardly think of it without a shudder.

VI.

I know not how long I could have withstood the shock which I daily experienced in that demoralized community. I was threatened with nervous prostration, and every hour I grew more feeble and more excited. At night, as I lay in my bed, in a small chamber under the gable-roof, where the frosty stars seemed to blink at me through the low window with cold, sharp eyes, I wondered why so miserable a sinner as I was permitted to live unpunished. And when the wintry wind was blowing and moaning under the eaves, I trembled where I lay; for it seemed to me that a just judgment was about to be visited upon me.

I can not but pity myself—though self-pity is a dangerous

thing—when I look back upon my youth. I can still remember my thoughts, my aspirations, my blind hopes, and the unsatisfied yearning that swelled my tender heart almost to bursting; and I know that I was not a bad boy, or certainly not the bad boy—the very bad and wicked boy—I imagined myself to be as I lay awake in that little chamber those dreary winter nights, and wished—yes, wished I had never been born!

Just at this time I received a letter from my paternal grandfather, who lived at a considerable distance from the old farm. Grandfather S—— in his letter, knowing that my vacation had come, wrote a most urgent invitation for me to visit him, and spend at least a portion of my holidays at his home. It seemed to me, poor little frightened fool that I was,—it seemed to me that it was my duty to stay and suffer the torture of the

"anxious seat" *because* it was
a torture; this very torture I
thought to be a proof of my
spiritual darkness.

Was it not my duty to remain
there, and try to be glad that
I was miserable, and miserably
paying the penalty of sin? Was
it not my duty to mortify myself
daily, to pass my nights in tears
and terror, until I had at last
experienced that incomprehen-
sible corporeal phenomenon,
"a change of heart"? Would it
not be doubly sinful in me to fly
from a place which had become
painful to me in consequence of
my imperfections, and seek peace
and happiness in the new home
to which I had been so cordially
bidden? I believed so, and for
this reason, and because I
wanted to do what was right
and for my best good, I secreted
the welcome letter and said
nothing of it to any one.

Grandfather F——, who knew
that I had received a letter, and

whose custom it was to read my correspondence, having waited a reasonable time for me to show him the letter, which I had put from me as a temptation and a snare, finally gravely demanded it, and I saw by his look that he thought me a dissembler. The letter was at once produced and read, when, to my joy, my grandfather embraced me and said, with a twinkle in his eye: "Why did you keep this from me?"

"Because," I replied, "I feared you would think me anxious to leave you and to get away from the 'Evangelist,' and so I was going to say nothing about it."

"You must go at once," he said, "to visit your Grandfather S——. He will think me selfish for having kept you from him so long. To-morrow you will start for his home, and remain so long as you find it agreeable."

I could hardly believe my senses; I could have clapped my

hands for joy; and yet, in the
midst of my anticipated escape
from the misery of the past
fortnight I felt guilty in feeling
no regret. The next day set me
free. I took an express train,
that fortunately stopped for a
moment at the village where I
had been so sorely perplexed;
and the afternoon saw me borne,
as upon the wings of the wind,
many miles away.

Oh, the relief that came to me
with every added moment! Oh,
the clouds that passed from
before my half-blinded eyes; the
millstones that fell from my
neck; the shadow that was
lifted from off my soul! It
seemed as if I must take wing,
also, and dash through space
in the delirious joy of my deliverance. And then, at intervals,
came a memory of those whom
I had left in the horrible atmosphere which so lately engulfed
me; and this memory was my
one regret.

VII.

My Grandfather S——was a Universalist; Grandfather F—— was not: he was a Presbyterian or a Congregationalist or a Baptist or a Methodist, or something; but which of them all I have never been quite sure. I could not help telling my new grandfather of my late experience with the "Evangelist"; for my heart was full of it, and sore because of it. I talked on and on, like a child who has a grievance; and while I was detailing my emotions—they were still very fresh and vivid—he arose and paced the floor excitedly. He said nothing in reply, though he listened attentively; when I had concluded he suddenly left the room in indignation. He was careful

never to drop a hint which
might lead me to think I had
been treated unwisely; but I
could not help observing that
my two grandfathers were very
far from being in sympathy, at
least as far as their respective
beliefs were concerned.

Sunday was not called the
"Sabbath" in this house; I was
now allowed to go to church
or stop away, as I thought
best. I was taken to a circus
for the first time in my life;
and I thought the graceful per-
formers, in their airy costumes,
but little lower than the
angels. My Sunday reading
was whatever I chose to make
it; I was encouraged to indulge
in a game of ball or marbles
on Sunday afternoon, and in
fair weather was driven about
the country to my complete
satisfaction. In fact, Sunday
was almost like a holiday, and
I no longer looked forward to
it with dread. I was as free as

a bird; and I was made much
of at the dinner table, where
the jovial Sunday guests took
their wine like old-school gentle-
men, and on several occasions
even toasted me with a pretty
compliment, which brought the
blush of pride to my cheek, and
a glance of genial patronage
from the kind eye of my host.

In the meetings, the Sunday
conferences, which my Grandfather S—— attended when he
felt so inclined, there was a light,
bustling air, very similar to that
which pervaded the Seminary
hall on Friday afternoon during
the declamation hour. I could
not help comparing it with the
unwholesome atmosphere which
prevailed in the "revival meetings" of the "Evangelist." I
had no longer a thought of fear,
nor of love either, nor of reverence, nor of anything in particular. In that community there
seemed to be a general under-
standing that all men are to be

saved, whether they will or no; that it is a waste of time trying to be wicked; it is, moreover, ill-bred and disagreeable, and one must submit to salvation in the end, notwithstanding. In short, with them man's chief end was to be sociable and satisfied.

Prayers were never heard in the house where I was then made welcome; nor grace at table; nor was there anything in the outward or inner life of the several members of the household that suggested the possibility of a final judgment. When I went to my room at night—which, by the by, I shared with a distant connection who was a sojourner there —a lad somewhat my senior,— I astonished my room-mate by kneeling at the bedside and silently repeating the prayer my mother had taught me.

It was a simple prayer and a brief one; and, though I could never be persuaded to omit it, somehow—I wonder how and why!—it always filled me with the deepest sadness. Was it because it was addressed aimlessly to the Deity, who was still in my mind the unintelligible Something beyond the stars? Was it because I had never known a direct answer to prayer? because I was beginning to distrust its efficacy? Or did the melancholy associations of the past cluster about it, and bring pain instead of easing it, and sorrow rather than relief?

I was daily gaining in health and spirits, and began to outgrow the morbid tendencies of my earlier years; yet often and often I perplexed myself with the vaguest speculations as to the cause of the wide difference between the lives of my two loved and respected ancestors.

VIII.

From this sportive bath—if I may so term it—in Universalism I returned to school. I was purged of much of the melancholy with which the "Evangelist" had imbued me. It seemed to me that since there were so many dissimilar creeds, and when even my own people differed widely in their faith, it mattered little what I believed myself, or, indeed, if I believed anything at all for the present. School-boy friendships consoled my heart; school holidays kept alive my interest in life. I was almost weaned from home, perhaps because I tried not to think of it any longer. When I thought of home I found it was still a sore spot that was touched; and so I gave myself up to the pleasures of the hour, and was all this time growing as a boy grows—right up like a weed, slender and frail.

When I had fully made up my mind that there was nothing to be done but patiently to await a summons to return, and had actually begun to care very little whether it came now or by and by, in the dim future, I was most unexpectedly called back to my far-away home beyond the sea. There was no especial occasion for this change at that time; I was quite contented, and might have continued so for a year or two longer. But a letter came bidding me pack up and set sail at once; and this I did almost immediately.

We were close upon the end of the school term; were all looking forward to the final exercises with great enthusiasm. As for me, I was expecting to distinguish myself at the closing

exhibition; and the frequent
rehearsals of a little drama in
which my schoolmates and I
were to appear had kept us for
some time in a state of delicious
excitement. Alas! I knew not
that I was to be taken from
school before the eventful day,
and that my part in the drama
—how I had dreamed of it night
after night!—was to be allotted
to another. I was not even to
have the satisfaction of being a
spectator on the brilliant night,
the proudest hour in the long
school year. It was necessary
for me to leave school suddenly,
in order to secure passage by a
ship in which family friends, in
whose charge I was placed,
were to embark.

My schoolmates, who had
shown me a thousand kind-
nesses, no sooner learned of my
intended departure than they,
with the aid of my teachers,
arranged a little farewell *fête* for
my especial delectation. This

was flattering indeed, and I endeavored to console myself as best I might, when, on a day sooner than was anticipated, my Grandfather F—— made his appearance, to take me home with him at once. He could not remain over for my sake; he could not conveniently return for me later; and, moreover, he had come at that very time for an especial purpose, and I was to accompany him without delay. I drove away with him in hot haste, with scarcely time to say farewell even to my bosom-friends; and, though I was silent, I was well-nigh heart-broken. Even the thought of setting forth so soon for the home I had vainly longed for could not compensate me in my double disappointment; I was in despair. And when I learned the cause of the good man's precipitous visit I fear I did him wrong; for my spirit was bitter and unforgiving.

With the earnest desire for my
spiritual welfare which he invariably evidenced, he had found,
as he believed, a favorable opportunity for impressing upon my
mind the solemn fact that death
is always with us, and that it
is our first duty to be prepared
for it. It seemed that a lad of
about my own age, but one
of whom I had never known
anything, had died suddenly:
it was to be present at his
obsequies, to take warning from
the awful suddenness of his
death, to listen to the lugubrious
wail of funeral hymns, to witness the agonizing grief of the
bereaved, that I was brought
away from the last embraces
of my loving mates.

Never shall I forget that scene.
The gloss of the rosewood coffin;
the sickly pallor of the memorial
wreaths (their odor is still per-
ceptible, and is forever associated
with   death)   the   brooding
thoughts of death—of death not

only of the body, but, as it seemed to me then, the possible death of the soul—of hope, of everything. The whining voice of the minister was at intervals drowned in the audible sobs of those who were gathered about that lifeless clay. What a hollow mockery it all seemed to me!

> I would not live alway,
> I ask not to stay,

sang the choir; but that marble image of youth, beauty, aspiration, and radiant love turned a deaf ear against the cruel sarcasm, and sealed its dimmed eye, as if in scorn of the singers of such foolish platitudes. Why should he not have lived always, thought I; or at least until he had learned to despise a world that had become hollow and hateful to him? What did that man, who stood droning at the head of the coffin, say to the inconsolable? What could he say to comfort those who were about to hide away forever that

marvellous effigy of sleep? What
could he or any one of them have
said to me that could for one
moment sweep away the blackness of darkness that was
enfolding my spirit like a pall?
They could say that he had been
saved from a wicked world,
whose wickedness he could not
yet have known; that he had
been snatched away from a life
in which he must have innocently revelled, for the bloom
of unsullied youth, the joy of
love, and the power of beauty
were his. They could say, and
they did say—at least the
preacher did—that he had gone
to his Maker. How did they
know that? What manner of
Maker was it who could undo
this miracle of life, who would
rob the world of its loveliness,
and leave the unseemly to wither
slowly in their dotage?

Oh, miserable that I was, and
without help! I heard only the
drawl of hopeless hymnody, the

half-apologetic interludes of the minister, the moan of those who refused to be comforted; I saw only the sharp outline of that white face; while over all and above all was the mingled odor of fresh varnish and tube-roses. There was the unceasing wonder in my soul why it was not I that was taken instead of that other one in the coffin yonder; for I had often been miserable enough to die.

When the earth had crashed brutally on the lid of the box in the grave, I could think only of the solitary soul that was, perchance, wandering somewhere, groping blindly and alone, seeking the presence of God. I could think only of the immeasurable loneliness it would find there; for the vast solitude of God was to me unutterably awful and overwhelming.

IX.

Once more I was in my own home and with my own people, after a long separation. We were living on the farther shore of a new land, among mixed races, in a city which has been called the most cosmopolitan in the United States. I was growing into the speculative age; had begun to philosophize after a fashion, and to analyze my own motives and those of others with whom I was brought in contact.

The state of unbelief in which so many whom I have known have complacently settled themselves has always seemed to me the most uncomfortable of all spiritual conditions; indeed, it is a condition which is totally wanting in spirituality. A firm conviction of some sort was absolutely necessary to my happiness. I felt that I *must* believe something. However, to tell the whole truth, it did not then seem to me to matter very much what I believed. I began a search after truth, or what I thought to be truth; and my search, at least, was an honest one. I knew God to be the source of all truth. I desired to worship Him; and, as He was worshiped after one fashion or another in the many and various churches of the city, I wandered from house to house like a weary spirit, seeking that absolute rest which I had never known.

My intellectual preferences led me to favor the Unitarians, who find a series of lectures, composed with literary elegance, and delivered with considerable oratorical grace, all that is necessary to the worship of God. I made the acquaintance of a

celebrated "divine," who professed no little interest in my
welfare. At his church the
musical adjuncts were highly
diverting, and for a while I was .
beguiled by the eloquent commonplaces of the minister, who
seldom failed to draw an exceed-
ingly well-dressed audience so
long as the fashionable season
lasted; at the close of it the
church doors were shut, and the
celebrated "divine" sought recreation at the seaside, in company
with the majority of his parish-
ioners. I· looked for fervor;
fervor seemed to me indispen-
sable to the love and the worship of God. I found it not.
The Unitarian, a superior being
who exchanges compliments
with his Creator, and whom
legions of angels can not abash—
the Unitarian offered me nothing
that I could take home with me,
locked up in my heart of hearts,
—not even a grain of comfort.

But the Methodist, clutching

his ponderous copy of the
Scriptures, swinging it above
his head with a shriek, while
many of his listeners responded
with audible "Amens"; and
then hurling the book upon the
pulpit, in which he roared like
a caged lion,—this was a mockery that sickened me. The
groans of auditors have never
aroused me to veneration, nor
does frenzy do more than
weaken my faith in the frenzied.

Between the Unitarian and the
various degrees of Methodism
I found nothing in the whole
range of Protestantism that did
not seem to me characterless,
colorless, almost formless,—the
poorest conceivable substitute
for worship in the true sense of
the term. What was the gathering together of men, women
and children once in seven
days to listen to the opinion
of a man on this text or that
text of Scripture, when I heard,
and could not avoid hearing, the

criticisms upon the discourse just delivered; the comments, favorable and unfavorable, made by those who considered their opinion as good as any man's? Nor could I help observing the worldly spirit which was everywhere and in a thousand ways evidenced with scarcely an attempt at disguise. It seemed to me that some *form* of worship was necessary; that there could be no true worship without form; that the mere herding of men, women and children under a "pastor" who told them what he knew, or thought he knew, concerning the word of God and its relation to the life that now is and that which is to come, profitable as it may be in some cases, *is not worship!* I saw no evidence of the presence of God in the building which they called the "house of God." Every symbol, every suggestion of Him and of His manifold attributes, was rigidly

excluded from the place dedi-
cated to Him. Even the choir
harmony, which should echo the
strains of the heavenly choir,
filling and thrilling us with the
most exalted reverence — the
choir rendered a class of music
which was calculated to dispel
every sentiment of devotion, and
to rob the exercises of the single
element of beauty left them.

Disheartened, I strayed one
evening into a church of the
Episcopal persuasion. Here I
found much—very much—that
was totally wanting elsewhere.
The somewhat meagre and
meaningless ceremonies were
conducted with an assumption
of dignified and respectful
reverence for something—for
what I could not exactly see. I
felt that the way was opened
a little for me. I was the most
willing and the most grateful
of novices, but I was destined to
suffer many a sad rebuff before
the end of my novitiate. In

vain did I strive to enter into
the spirit of that faith: to me
it was spiritless and cold; its
forms were formal; and though
the prayers are of unrivalled
beauty, and the litanies—of
Catholic origin—won upon me
like the mystical refrain of some
antique temple worship; though
the music was spiritually elevat-
ing, and the architecture a
suitable setting for it all, I felt
at last that this was a form
indeed, but an almost meaningless form; a form without spirit
or substance. So I turned from
the Episcopal Church, satisfied
that it is feebly though expen-
sively nourished by a severely,
not to say frigidly, polite community,—a community meagre
in numbers, but of unquestion-
able taste.

It was my custom to revisit
in turn the houses of these
several denominations, striving
always to reconcile myself to
observances at which I in-

stinctively rebelled. I was
constantly laboring under the
conviction that if my heart was
not touched it was because
of the hardness of the heart;
and that the fault, of whatever
nature it might be, was mine
alone.

Once, and once only, I suffered
myself to be enticed into a public
hall where "Moody and Sankey"
were holding forth to a mob of
ill-bred and irreverent people.
I entered that hall in a spirit of
honest inquiry; I was open to
conviction, and had, for the time
at least, dismissed all prejudice
from my mind. It was the hour
of noon. These meetings were
held in the business quarter of
the town, for the especial benefit
of business men. The public in
general, but business men in
particular, were invited somewhat ostentatiously (by means
of placards in large type, dis-
tributed upon the street-corners
and posted upon the walls)

to go to —— Hall, —— street, and
"*find Jesus*," from 12 to 1 p. m.,
daily! The intense vulgarity of
the proceedings, to say nothing
of the blasphemy that prevailed,
filled me with disgust; the
horror I experienced when subjected to the baleful influences
of the illiterate itinerant "Evangelist" returned in such force
that I hastened from the place
in dismay. Nearly every Protestant denomination in the
city was represented there.
Messrs. Moody and Sankey
created an excitement which all
of them combined would fail
to do; but by countenancing
Messrs. Moody and Sankey, the
local ministry could at the close
of the season step in and divide
the spoils; the converts were
parcelled out among them, and
the excitement subsided.

Thus the Protestant Church,
in its innumerable branches, lent
its aid to the Evangelists, and
met for the only time on neutral

ground; yet it is but a few steps from the temporary insanity of Messrs. Moody and Sankey's emotional victims to the appalling blasphemies of the "Salvation Army." I resolved never again to enter a Protestant church; never again to seek to reconcile her multifarious denominational differences; never again to imperil the little peace of mind I had by profitless speculation.

X.

And now came the strangest experience of all. One day I received a letter from a lady who was personally unknown to me, though I knew and had long known her by reputation. She was a conspicuous character; she lectured regularly, on Sundays, in one of the theatres, usually upon a popular topic and in a popular vein, and succeeded in arresting the attention of the large audiences which she drew together week after week.

I had for some time been contributing to various magazines and journals; and, doubtless as much in consequence of my youth as for any literary merit which my juvenile productions betrayed, I had won a kind of romantic local reputation,

which I have since wondered
was not my ruin. Had I cared
more for what the public
thought of me than for what
I longed to think of myself, I
should hardly have escapéd the
vainglory that dazzles and con-
founds so many precocious
amateurs.

This lady begged to know me;
entreated me to call upon her,
and promised me the sort of
entertainment which she must
have known would be most
acceptable to a callow poet. I
was, of course, much flattered,
and very willingly visited her.
She lived in a suburban cottage,
in the midst of a small but
luxuriant garden. Within that
modest home I found repose;
surrounded by every element of
feminine refinement, we seemed
far removed from the weary
world, and, for a period, our
intercourse was very grateful
to me.

Her voice was low and sweet,

and her manner was singularly gentle and winning. It was said of her by the enthusiasts who noisily proclaimed her virtues that she led a nun's life, and that her days were passed in meditation and in acts of silent charity. She certainly seemed to me one of the most exalted natures with which I had ever been brought in contact. The praise she gave me was enthusiastic but discriminating; the sympathy she showed me won the confidence and gratitude of my heart. She exacted, without so much as asking it, an unconditional surrender. She was what is popularly known as an "inspirational speaker"; her lectures were seldom prepared beforehand, and never written or memorized; on the impulse of the moment she spoke with amazing volubility and brilliancy. She was an earnest, constant and appreciative reader; hers was a poetic tem-

perament, and she was easily
moved to tears; her natural
gaiety was tempered by a memory of the sorrow and disap-
pointments with which her life
had been filled; and, withal, she
was possessed of a profound,
intuitive knowledge of human
nature. Is it any wonder that
I flew to her in my desponding
moods, or that she found in me
an interesting and interested
votary?

It was her custom to entertain
me with discourses upon the
supernatural. Often, with closed
eyes, or a look fixed on vacancy,
she would pour forth volumes
of eloquent mysticism, to which
I listened in rapt wonderment.
In her presence I began to feel
the influence of which she so
often spoke. It seemed to me
that the little parlor in which
we sat, in a kind of artificial
twilight that was quite its own,
was the most serenely beautiful
of retreats. I almost believed

that the good spirits she professed to see, and with whom
she apparently held converse,
were really near me; that they
were in many ways ministering
to me; that I was no longer
alone in my earthly pilgrimage,
for those invisible ambassadors
—her vassals—were in my confidence, and were no more to
leave me, night or day.

Often she gave me messages
that thrilled me with hope and
joy; always they were such as
I longed to hear repeated; and
in no case did they fail to assure
me, in one form or another, of
the necessity of my seeking them
and trusting them and their
interpreter—the mysterious lady
through whose lips they spoke,
and in whose mediumship they
found the fullest expression. By
her I was slowly led through all
the phases of that dangerous
doctrine known as "Spiritual-
ism," in which so many noble
natures have become hopelessly

involved. With her I underwent
the ordeal of the test of faith;
the whole range of supernatural
phenomena was thrown open
to me; my ears heard, my eyes
saw, my fingers touched the
objects which were unaccountably produced for my delectation, and which speedily and
unaccountably vanished from
my sight. I was in ecstasy; I
was ready—nay, eager to accept
all things, believe all things,
hope all things of the future, in
which I was assured the new
faith would be the salvation of
the world. It was not until the
grossest deceptions had been
practised upon me that my faith
began to question. I believed
blindly, because it was an easy
and comforting belief; but
having lost faith in one phase
of this deluding mystery, my
faith was shaken in it all, and
I believed no more. Like a
house built upon sand, one wave
swept it to destruction; and

then, and not till then, she who
had been my guide, philosopher
and friend; who had counselled
me in my perplexity, comforted
me in sorrow, and whom I
thought to be the pattern of all
the virtues, — she proved to be
a priestess among the modern
pagans, and an advocate of
their unholy and lascivious rites.

XI.

Thrown rudely back upon myself, having by this time lost confidence in everybody and everything, there was still in my heart the yearning after the unattainable. I dreamed more than ever; indeed, my life was more than half a dream. I wondered why, in the whole wide world, there was no form of religion such as I felt the absolute need of, and without which I was as one cast away in the desert. Then in my imagination I erected the altar before which I longed to prostrate myself in tender devotion. It was my intention secretly to set up a tabernacle in my chamber—a place of sacrifice, to which I might enter alone and unobserved, and there offer the prayer which was ever in my

heart and often upon my lips.
Adjoining my chamber was
a closet, lighted by a rose-
window; this would admirably
answer my purpose; the glass
of the window could be stained
so that a beautiful and unearthly glow would suffuse the
place; the walls, hung with rich
draperies, were to enclose me
as with curtains of cloud; the
ceiling would be of azure, starred
with golden stars; the floor
cushioned deep with velvet rugs,
on which to kneel in the hour of
my retreat. There was to be an
altar white as the new-fallen
snow,—an altar decorated with
the emblems of death and im-
mortality; an altar gilded and
draped with lace, and having
tapers upon it, which were to
be lighted whenever I entered
that sanctuary. I wanted these
tapers to be many, and I wished
that they might burn forever;
for they were to stand before a
shrine with golden doors, which

doors were to be kept closed, save only when I could open them in a spirit of unspeakable reverence.

I could never, even in imagination, furnish that shrine with sufficient splendor. I wanted the loveliest light to radiate from the holy of holies when I bowed before it with a broken and a contrite heart; for therein was to be enshrined the image of the Son of God, while all about were choirs of chanting Cherubim and Seraphim, and in the midst thereof the Holy Spirit hovering in the form of a white dove. Fresh flowers were to breathe fragrance in the ceaseless serenity of this temple; balsams and frankincense and myrrh were to smoulder there in brasiers and tripods. I was to put the shoes from off my feet and to bathe and to put on a suitable garment before I entered this to me most sacred, as it was the most secret, of chambers. No eye save mine was to behold it; no ear to have any knowledge of it whatever; for the world I had trusted had betrayed me, and I now sought only to be alone with God in the temple I had builded for His sake. Such was my dream,— a dream never to be realized.

XII.

The love of music was with me a passion. Melody soothed me in excitement, and aroused me from periods of lethargy to healthful spiritual and mental activity. My music-master, a German enthusiast, had often spoken to me of his choir and organ, and of the classical masters whose creations it was his delight to render.

There was to be, on some high festival in the church of which he was musical director, a very famous composition produced, with an efficient chorus and full orchestral accompaniment; and my master urged me to be present on that occasion, promising me a seat by his side near the organ. I met him at the door of the cathedral; it was with difficulty that we made our

way to the organ-loft, so dense
was the throng that had long
since filled the pews, galleries,
and aisles, and so great the
crowd in the vestibule and upon
the steps and pavement before
the cathedral doors. From my
position by the organist, above
the heads of the singers and
instrumentalists, I looked into
the mystic nave, and saw the
high altar with its constellations
of twinkling tapers, and the
soft glow of the lesser lights
upon the altars in the transepts.
I saw the glorious paintings,
the exquisite statues, and the
admirable   architectural   sur-
roundings; and, though I could
not but recur with some slight
taint of suspicion to my early
experience in the chapel opposite
the old homestead, I had devel-
oped sufficient self-composure
carefully to survey and heartily
to admire all I saw and heard.

At last I beheld a congregation that shared a single senti-

ment; the whole body seemed
swayed by one emotion, yet
each member of that vast body
was individually absorbed in a
private devotion. Where else
had I seen such an impressive
spectacle, where else such rever-
ent decorum? Where else *could*
I have seen it? I was deeply
moved; and when my master
touched the keys of his instru-
ment, and a prelude as delicate
and as full of inspiration as the
song of the soaring lark was
breathed among the stately pipe
columns that towered almost
like a forest above ou. heads;
when the long procession of
acolytes entered and, bowing
before the tabernacle, ranged
themselves within the altar-
railing; when the deacons and
priests followed, preceding the
bishop in his rich robes; when
the solemn ceremonials were
in progress, and the incense-
clouded air trembled with the
gush of melody that seemed

to permeate the very stones of
the edifice and to sway that
mass of humanity as the tide is
swayed slowly to and fro; when
every heart seemed to respond
to a single pulse—a pulse throb-
bing in one great heart that was
burning with the love of God:
when I began to realize this I
held my breath and prayed that
the ecstasy of that hour might
never end. It was a mighty
mystery that struck me dumb
with awe!

Of the inclinations, salutations
and genuflections; of the vesting
and unvesting; the cap and
mitre, the cruets, incense-boats
and censers; of the candles,
torches, missals; the ablutions
and chiming bells; of the deep,
ominous silence that fell upon
us at intervals; the elevations,
the thrice solemn administration of the Sacrament, and the
sublime benediction, I knew
nothing, and less than nothing;
for I doubtless misinterpreted

very much of all that I saw and heard. But to see and to hear was enough, and more than enough: my hungering and thirsting soul was fed with spiritual manna; it could no longer content itself with husks.

My master, who had been absorbed in his professional duties, turned to me when he at last lifted his hands from the organ. The great building was nearly empty; a few worshipers still knelt in the body of the church, or were grouped before the several altars; two sanctuary boys were carefully and deliberately extinguishing the tapers upon the altar; a priest was kneeling within the railing, and everywhere still floated the faint, blue filmy clouds that sweetened the air, so that it seemed to have blown softly from the gardens of paradise!—and my master turned to me! I could not speak; I felt that my cheeks were colorless; and, as we walked away from the cathedral door, and were parting at the street corner, he said to me: "Well! will you come again?"

Come again! My ideal temple, my dream-sanctuary, with its crude and feeble symbolism, had crumbled into ruins and utterly vanished before this august reality. This was reality indeed; and it was a reality of whose majesty I was fully conscious, though as yet I knew absolutely nothing of its marvellously beautiful significance. Would I come again? I nodded my head in token of assent; yet at that moment something within me seemed to struggle against it and to raise a question of doubt. Is there anything in the wide world more tenacious of life than an inherited prejudice?

XIII.

I did go again and again, and yet again. A seat was always reserved for me in the organ-loft, and from that serene and curtained seclusion I witnessed the Holy Sacrifice of the Mass, until I began to grow familiar with its forms, at least, and to long earnestly to comprehend their signification. Our maid at home was a Catholic, but she had never in any way sought to influence me in favor of her religion; nor was she aware that I was in the habit of attending Mass and Vespers when so inclined.

The faith of my people was dying out or growing luke-warm. What was there to call them to a church, if the minister chanced not to be an agreeable speaker? They were liberal

Protestants, growing more and
more liberal from year to year;
and they followed the majority
in the track of the sensational
pulpit orator—the favorite of
the hour. Even family prayers
had become infrequent, and we
children, grown now to the
years of discretion, attended
them or not as we saw fit.
Grace at table was often
omitted or forgotten; and, I
suppose, the natural, the inevi-
table tendency of Protestantism
was as evident in my home as
in any Protestant home of to-
day, and no more evident than
it is and must be everywhere.

The stubborn prejudices which
I found it difficult to eradicate,
and which they still clung to,
were what led them to visit
a church at intervals; and in
most cases they did so in
a critical or curious mood,
rather than in a spirit of reverence or from a sense of duty.
They knew at this time that it

was my custom to attend the Catholic church, but thought that I went only to listen to the choir; and, though they sometimes asked me if I would like to hear this or that preacher in whom they were for the time being interested, they never urged me to accompany them, and made no objection to my seeking salvation in any way that I saw fit.

I was groping in the dark when a little light threw a ray across my path, suddenly, unexpectedly, as if a star had fallen. One day, on the mantel-piece in our dining-room,—shall I ever forget that mantel, or the corner of it on which the wee book in its brown paper cover was lying!—I found a copy of "The Poor Man's Catechism." I had never before seen a Catholic catechism, nor any Catholic book whatever; but we had stores of anti-Catholic works, and the discovery of this little spy in the camp somewhat startled me. I at once took it away to my chamber and began to read it.

I was on my guard when I turned the first pages of that homely little pamphlet; it was a poor and ragged thing, by no means calculated to prepossess any one in its favor. I was even inclined to be antagonistic when I began to read; but the simplicity and truth that shone from every page disarmed me; the plain, direct questions and the plain, direct answers were just such as I had been longing to ask and to receive. Here they were in my own hands, to be asked as often as I chose, and answered immediately and always. I became profoundly interested; I could not lay down the little oracle till I had gone through it two or three times over. I read it first with curious interest; and afterward reread it, to make sure that I had read it aright; then read again, to clear some obscure point or to get the full meaning of certain passages. What a reading was that when, finally, I read it slowly and earnestly, asking myself after each separate answer, "Can you believe this?" "Do you believe it?" After each and all of those answers I answered, and I answered triumphantly, "I can and I do!"

I resolved to become a Catholic at once; I supposed that I had only to say as much and I should immediately find the doors of the Mother Church thrown wide open and the stray sheep admitted into the fold without question. This is probably the impression which prevails among non-Catholics. I have heard of those who have been made Catholics almost before they knew it, and possibly without their full consent; as if one might be caught and branded, and then turned loose again, the property of a new owner. I have always heard this from non-Catholics, and no doubt they believed what they were saying.

The question with me was to whom was I to offer myself, now that my path was made straight? In the wide circle of my friends and acquaintances there was not one Catholic that I knew of,—my music-master professed nothing. Our maid had said to me, "Go to the priest!" Good soul, she little knew that I had never spoken to one, and was still half afraid of them, one and all. Now, for me to go boldly to the priest's door and knock, asking to be admitted and adopted, required more moral courage than I was possessed of; and so the weeks and months passed by, I going regularly to Mass, and timidly, no doubt awkwardly, crossing myself with holy water; for I believed it was not wrong for me to do this much, even if I were not yet a Catholic.

One day I stole cautiously into a Catholic bookstore, and, after a great deal of hesitation (for I was divided between desire and distrust), I selected and purchased a fine large crucifix, which I secreted under my coat and conveyed privately to my chamber. It was a long time before any member of my family was aware that I had that precious crucifix in my possession. I was afraid to tell them; but why I was afraid I know not; perhaps I was afraid of being laughed at, and of having *it* ridiculed. Oh, how happy was I with it, when the whole truth was out at last! I *was* laughed at for my superstition, but I smothered my grief and indignation; I held my peace. I hung the blessed symbol of our Redemption upon the wall above my bed, and prayed there night

and morning as I had never
prayed before.

How was I to begin to be
a Catholic?—that was the
question that I asked myself
every hour in the day. Often I
knelt in the church during day
or evening, hoping some one
would discover my anxiety by
a sign and come to my relief.
Often I went to the very door
of the priests' house, and hung
about there, not daring to
knock, but trusting that I
should ultimately attract the
attention of the priests, and be
met at least half way. I was
always talking of the Church,
stupidly and ignorantly, no
doubt, but with honest enthusiasm; frequently I was ridiculed
for my pains; and thus the time
passed, and I was no nearer the
longed-for goal than at the hour
when I first opened the little
brown pamphlet that helped me
take the first step toward
Truth.

That Catechism I kept, and
I have it still; I had a right to
keep it, for none of us was ever
able to ascertain when or how
it came into the house. No
owner was ever found for it, and
no one knew who placed it upon
the mantel. When it came into
my possession I was the only
one who had seen it or had
knowledge of it.

XIV.

A certain lady of liberal tendencies who had published several books, and whose house was the resort of all classes of people, had made much of me — yet not enough to spoil me. The favoritism which she did not hesitate to show me at all times and in all places had given me no little distinction in her very extensive and by no means exclusive social circle.

Had it been possible for me to content myself with mere applause, it is probable that I might never have been more than an enthusiastic though ingenuous admirer of the external beauty of the Catholic Church; but the craving of my heart, that drove me, yea even starved me, out of Protestantism, and left me to seek relief in many and various quarters, was not to be satisfied with this alone. I accepted gratefully whatever worldly consolation— and it was of the earth, earthy— my friend could offer me; met many strange and interesting people in her society, and was no doubt diverted for the time; but desire never failed me, and when I had gone out from her presence I was immediately disinterested and disturbed.

On one occasion when, in wandering aimlessly about the town, I found myself in the vicinity of my friend's house, I resolved to enter and pass an idle hour with her. She was at home, was receiving a solitary guest—a lady whom I had never before met. I was of course presented, and the conversation, which my entrance had interrupted for a moment, was resumed. I forget the subject of that conversation; I remember nothing of all that was said,

save that some careless witti-
cism of the hostess concerning
what she was pleased to call the
"saint-worship" of the Catholic
Church aroused my ire. I
remember that I said to her,
somewhat hotly: "Have you
no reverence for that glorious
type of womanhood, the Blessed
Virgin?" I believe that she had,
and was quick to acknowledge
it; but immediately the other
lady who was present turned
to me and asked: "Are you a
Catholic?" Without hesitation,
though I knew nothing of her
or of her faith, I replied, half
defiantly: "No, but I should like
to be." The hostess laughed
gaily at my earnest manner,
and the subject was skilfully
dropped. It might all have
ended there; but, please God,
it was not to end; it was
rather a beginning, and the
best beginning I had yet made.

When I rose to take my leave,
the lady rose also, and together

we passed out into the street. There she asked me if I would walk her way; and thus I came to accompany her to her house, which was not far distant. Meanwhile this brief dialogue was all that passed between us:

"Do you really desire to become a Catholic?"

"Of all things, Madame, it is this I most desire."

"Then, why do you not place yourself under the instruction of some priest?"

"Because I have never had the happiness of knowing one."

"I can very easily make you acquainted with my confessor, who is to visit me to-morrow afternoon at two o'clock. If you would like to meet him, come here, to my house, at that hour, and I will present you."

At last I felt that my hand was upon the latch of the door, at which I had been vainly knocking for so long and so weary a time.

XV.

The name of this good lady I
have forgotten; indeed I saw her
only twice, and I never knew
anything of her history or her
fate. The house where she then
lived I still remember, and I
have watched it through its
many vicissitudes with a kind of
personal interest such as I have
felt for few houses. It has been
tenanted by all sorts and conditions of men; was sometimes
tenantless, with a placard hung
in the uncurtained window; and
again the windows would be
thronged with children's faces,
and the halo of happiness was
over it all. Finally, it has become one of several similar
buildings, swarming with rustics
and day-laborers, who find in
this little colony (known under
the general name of somebody's

Temperance Hotel) extraordi-
narily cheap board and lodging
per day, week, and month.

When I went to the house at
the appointed hour, I was
shown into a pretty parlor,
where a fine engraving of Pope
Pius IX., of blessed memory,
filled the place of honor upon the
walls, and all the pictures were
of a sacred character. The
hostess was looking anxiously
for the arrival of the priest; she
began to fear that he might not
come at all, for his duties were
onerous though grateful, and he
might at the last moment have
been summoned to the bedside of
the sick or the dying. He came
when we had quite despaired of
his coming. He had been called
away, and had hastened to meet
us, if only for a moment, inas-
much as the lady, who feared
that something might prevent
him, had sent him word of my
desire to meet and confer with
him on an important question.

He was a modest, almost
diffident young priest, not very
long in orders, and was one of
several who were stationed in
one of the most populous
parishes in the city. He looked
weary and worn, but was cheerful, and had even a subdued,
boyish gayety that charmed me
and soon put to flight all the
embarrassment which I otherwise might have experienced;
and he easily won my confidence.
I felt that we were to be fast
friends; and yet the clerical cut
of his garb, and the peculiar and
undefined reserve — which is a
characteristic of the clergy,—
reminded me always that I was
for the first time in my life face
to face with one of those beings
who had been the horror of my
infant years.

What did he say to me? I
hardly know; we talked of everything but religion. We laughed
and joked, and were shortly as
cosy as possible; and then he

abruptly took his leave, for he had still many things to do. The atmosphere of that little parlor seemed sweeter and more peaceful for his presence; and even in his absence something of that sweetness and serenity remained.

It was agreed that I was to visit him on the evening following. I was to await him in the chapel of his parish as he came from the confessional; and I impatiently looked forward to that hour, for the young priest had no sooner left me than I wished him back again. He was, in truth, perfectly new to me, and unlike any one whom I had ever known. On the morrow, then, in the chapel, I was to await him at the confessional. How the knowledge of this would have chilled the marrow in the bones of my respective grandsires! Neither of them ever knew it, for both of them died soon after.

XVI.

Dear little dingy chapel! how
dark you were that night! and
how dark the street, with the
wind and the rain driving
against my face, as I went in
search of you!

That night I chanced to run
across a friend, who turned to
walk with me. Him I had to
get rid of in some way, but
how? I told him I had an
engagement, and his fraternal
curiosity (for we were intimates)
was at once aroused. To satisfy
him I resorted to invention.
(How delicately I am putting it
now; for, to be plain with you,
it was a falsehood I told him!)
Was it shame, false shame, that
persuaded me to keep my inter-
view a secret, and encouraged
me in deliberately misleading
him? Ought I not to have

gloried in the step I was about
to take, though I took it almost
blindly, and alone, and in the
darkest of dark nights? My
friend left me in perplexity, for
I fear there was guilt in my
voice. But he did not leave me
till I had led him past the door
of the chapel and quite out of
my way; then I made the circuit
of the square, and coming again
to the chapel door, which stood
invitingly open, I looked up and
down the street, which was
deserted at the moment, and
then quietly stole within.

Dear little dingy chapel, that
has given place — though not
without rivers of tears from the
hearts that knew and loved you
—to the stately edifice, with its
chimes of joy-bells far aloft in
the great, high tower!

A single lamp burned like a
golden star before the altar and
the Blessed Sacrament; two or
three glimmering lights threw a
feeble ray in the far corners of

the chapel, where groups of
penitents were crouching near
the confessionals. What an
unearthly stillness was there!
I looked with awe upon those
who were humbling themselves
before Him unto whom is given
the power to loose and to bind
sin. I listened, with beating
heart, to the low mutter of lips
within the curtained niches; the
noiseless stir of the screen that
hid the confessor from view
thrilled me. When would my
turn come to enter that dim
retreat and pour out my
iniquities at the feet of those
servants of God? When might
I arise from there with a clean
heart and a spirit whiter than
snow? I knelt in the chapel,
lost in a vague reverie, wondering if I had yet a right to kneel
there; wondering how they feel
who go in and come out from
under the drapery of the confessional; wondering if the
quenchless star whose pale

beam falls forever upon the golden doors of the tabernacle might not dart one ray into the dim chamber of my heart and illumine it forever.

A hand touched me lightly upon the shoulder. I turned: it was the young priest, now clad in the long, dark robe which was the horror of my childhood; but I had overcome all fear, and, full of trust, I rose and followed him. As we passed before the Blessed Sacrament the young priest prostrated himself for a moment; the impulse to follow his example was irresistible. We arose together, and entered a door that admitted us to a passage connecting the chapel with the priests' house.

I was taken into a small study walled with books, and was there, in the kindest spirit, carefully and freely questioned. Never before had I realized how little I knew of the great scheme

of salvation. I was to begin at
the beginning, for I had everything to learn; and yet it
is probable that I knew as
much of Catholicism as any
Protestant, and possibly I knew
far more than most of them.

We looked over many volumes
in that library; the history, the
philosophy, the poetry of the
Church was gradually laid open
to me. I felt as if I were
entering a new world—a world
full of mysterious beauty and
fascination. I felt that I could
never learn enough of this
marvellous Church—never begin
to know as much of it as I
should know; but what perplexed me more than all was
the false knowledge which I
had to unlearn, the cruel mis-
statements which had to be
corrected, and the latent, inborn
prejudices which I must needs
root out and trample underfoot.

More than once that evening
we were interrupted: poor men

and poor women came to lay their troubles before this youthful Father. What a world of care was his! It was a word of advice or encouragement to one; a little substantial aid to another; a willing promise to do this or that for a third— enough, it seemed to me, to tax the strength of the stoutest, and to keep a dozen busy for days to come.

This was his daily life. Rest he never knew; weariness he discountenanced; famine and pestilence he feared not; himself the servant of servants, worthy indeed of his hire, was unremunerated in a profession exacting to a degree, of unceasing activity, and peculiarly circumscribed and exclusive.

Above us was a small, plainly furnished chamber; within it there was a bed, which was neat and clean and hard; a crucifix also, and a few pious pictures; a holy-water font, and an

uncushioned *prie-dieu*. Thither
he repaired at a late hour, seeking the brief sleep allotted him.
He did not leave me that night
till I had reluctantly withdrawn,
taking with me several works
of a controversial character,
which I was to "read, mark,
learn, and inwardly digest";
and then exchange them for
others, which were at my
disposal.

Of all the ministers whom I
had met, where had I found one
worthy to be compared with
this modest young priest? He
immediately won my esteem,
and I resolved to visit him as
often as I might without
intrusion. Alas! he was almost
immediately removed to some
distant country parish, and him
I never saw again, nor heard
of more.

XVII.

The young priest in his unexpected departure had not been unmindful of me: I could still exchange books at the library in the priests' house whenever I chose to; and I was made acquainted with a Catholic lady, who, in turn, made me known to the Jesuit Fathers at St. Ignatius' College. All went smoothly now; and it was with a sense of absolute relief that I saw myself welcomed by the wise and powerful yet humble Order whose very name is a bugbear in the ears of Protestants and unbelievers. One of the Reverend Fathers, a grand old man, was to take full charge of me. I knew always where to seek him, found him at all times accessible, and between us there sprang

up an affectionate familiarity
that was uninterrupted until his
death.

Spirit of my beloved preceptor
—the shadow of whose sublime
countenance, still hanging upon
my wall, now refreshes my
memory,—O desert me not! but
from the serenity of thy sacred
sphere lead me and direct me
as thou wert wont to do when
my feet stumbled and my heart
was faint.

It was Father A——, of the
Society of Jesus, who made my
perplexing studies a delight. It
was to him I confided the last
vestige of the inborn prejudice
which so tenaciously clung to
me. It was he who said to
me, "Read what you will, so
long as you read earnestly and
honestly the books I give you."
At that time I read many anti-
Catholic works,—probably at
least one for every Catholic
book the good Father gave me.
More than once I went to the

doors of Protestant churches, intending to give them a final trial; but my revulsion was so great that I was forced to turn from them, feeling that at last I had burst the bonds of their bigoted and ignorant prejudice.

I believe any reasonable man can not read in connection a Catholic and an anti-Catholic work without discovering the logical truth of the one and the false premises of the other. Childish and stupid seem to me the arguments of the Protestants; empty, vulgar and worthless the tirades of infidels and fanatical writers. I would not recommend any Catholic to read aught of those; they are vanity and vexation of spirit; they are full of subtle poison, that robs the heart of rest, of health, of hope—of everything. A single page of plausible falsehood may pervert an unprejudiced mind so that a whole volume of truth will hardly restore it; therefore leave them alone.

Protestants may fortify themselves with the bulk of their best known treatises, and believe themselves secure; but let them read standard Catholic writers; these books will be volumes of revelation to them. Let them carefully compare all, and I venture to assert, if the readers be of sound judgment, they will soon lean joyfully toward the Mother Church, and do so with a heart full of pity and amazement at the magnitude of the Protestant and infidel misconception of the truths of that venerable Church.

About this time one of my chosen friends—I might almost say my bosom-friend—was a popular young Protestant minister. We were so intimate that he could not but see the drift of my thoughts; and it was no doubt with horror that he noted the gradual development of my love and reverence for, and my growing trust in, a doctrine which was in his eyes an abomination. I had been very fond of him, for we had much in common: our tastes in music, art and literature were one, and we were usually swayed by a single emotion. It was a rare and beautiful friendship. He was young, enthusiastic, refined, with a singularly winning manner; yet I could not but compare his worldly condition with that of the youthful priest—the first I met—and of my venerable Jesuit Father. It is true, the latter was one of an Order possessed of great wealth and influence, yet the private apartment of my Reverend Father was a bare cell; and I remember that beside his Breviary and his rosary he had no earthly possessions, not even an album to hold the half-dozen photographs some friends had sent him. And yet he had been of a noble family in Italy, possessed of a vast fortune, which he poured into the coffers of the church-charities; and his early life had been passed at the brilliant court of Naples in the palmy days of that reign.

But no—I had forgotten; he was the possessor of an ebony snuff-box, bearing a medallion of the Madonna upon the cover. O Father A——! Father A——! may you be pardoned this solitary extravagance by the revilers of your holy Order! I know beyond question that your purse was always light.

My ministerial friend, on the other hand, being a handsome bachelor, and "a great catch," occupied a suite of rooms in the house of one of the most fashionable members of his congregation. His study was a *boudoir*, filled with æsthetic bric-a-brac; his chamber a triumph of elegant upholstering. He had numerous albums, richly

bound, and filled with the finest
specimens of the photographer's
art. Constantly in the receipt
of dinner and social invitations,
tokens of esteem, bouquets, and
all manner of flattering atten-
tions, he—poor, puzzled boy—
seemed to pass a good portion
of his time in laying up em-
broidered slippers and smoking-
caps—the handiwork of young
lady admirers—against the
rainy day of his declining
popularity. We were frequently
together at one time, but the
day came when he felt that he
must save me from taking the
step I was meditating; and,
after a long, wordy and heated
argument, we parted in coldness; and the coldness, very
naturally grew apace—it grew
till I ultimately lost sight of
him entirely.

Meanwhile I had been dili-
gently prosecuting my studies,
and in my frequent and lengthy
interviews with Father A——

had begun to see my way clearly, to walk firmly in the path he led me, and to cling steadfastly to the one hope of being received into the Church. I felt it reasonable and proper that I should make known to my parents the sole desire of my heart, and one day I did so. We were sitting together, after dinner, in the cosy library. My father, who had been reading aloud to us, laid down his book, and, not knowing exactly where or how to begin, I was out with the whole truth at once. I said, abruptly, "I have resolved to join the Catholic Church"; and there I paused. For some time we were all silent; then my mother spoke: "I trust that you will not hastily take any step that you may hereafter have cause to regret."—"I am not taking it hastily," said I; "I have been thinking of it for a very long time, and I am satisfied that my only happiness

rests in it." Then my father
added: "You are old enough to
reason for yourself and with
yourself, but I would advise
you to consider well before you
have gone too far."

We were all sadder that evening than we had been before,
and there were tears in my
mother's eyes when I kissed her
good-night; but the subject was
never again mentioned among
us. A few days later Father
A—— said to me: "Whom will
you choose for godfather?" I
actually knew no one to turn to
in this emergency, and so Father
A—— added: "I can bring you
one who will do you honor; you
will be baptized in the baptistery of the cathedral at two
o'clock on Saturday next."

XVIII.

It was a strange, eventful season for me of which I now write. I could not close my eyes on the night preceding my baptism, and when Saturday came I was nervous and depressed. Of course I had never been baptized (my parents did not believe in infant baptism); and, as the palpable "change of heart" had never caused me much uneasiness — somehow my heart would not or could not change,—a Protestant baptism had never seemed to me a necessary means of grace, and I had lived on and on without fear of mortal sin.

A little before two o'clock on the appointed day I entered the cathedral. Sunshine was flooding the nave with a rich, mellow light; some one was

noiselessly wreathing the high
altar with fresh flowers. Without the sombre walls was the
rumble of the great city; within
was a holy and unutterable
peace; but my heart beat wildly
and would not be quieted. I
heard footsteps approaching as
I knelt before the altar, and
the next moment Father A——
was kneeling by my side, in
silent prayer. Presently he
turned and whispered to me,
and we quietly withdrew to
the baptistery. My emotions
were indescribable. A gentleman who was with Father
A——was made known to me;
he was to be my godfather. He
was a distinguished convert, the
author of a remarkably able and
logical volume entitled "The
Path which Led a Protestant
Lawyer into the Catholic
Church."

Under the beautifully tinted
window of the baptistery stood
the white marble font. But let

me confess at once that throughout the administration of that
most solemn sacrament I was
filled with an awe that dulled
rather than quickened my
senses. No one was present
save us three and an assistant.
I was carefully and tenderly
directed to the end, and then
my emotions became uncontrol-
lable, and, throwing myself on
the breast of my godfather,
who, with Father A——, affec-
tionately embraced me, I shed
floods of tears.

We returned to the altar, and
there, kneeling between these
spiritual and temporal advisers,
I laid my heart in absolute
surrender. From the steps of
that altar I seemed to rise a
new being. I had shattered the
chrysalis, and the wings of my
soul expanded in the everlasting
light that radiates from the
Throne of Grace. They left me
there. I was glad to be alone;
a great calm had fallen upon

me, and I feared lest even the most friendly of voices might trouble or dispel it. When I passed into the street, I kept saying to myself: "I am a Catholic! I am a Catholic at last!" And it seemed to me then as if my eyes were just opening upon another and a better world.

XIX.

Did any one ever approach
the mysterious portal of the
confessional for the first time
without a feeling of awe?
My turn came at last. It was
on a night when many penitents
were gathered in the dimly-
lighted chapel. For a time I
held aloof, not knowing exactly
what to do nor how to do it.
Of course the formula and the
instructions were in my prayer-
book—I had long since purchased a prayer-book,—but I felt
awkward and half afraid; and
so I knelt apart from the others,
and patiently awaited my turn.

People came and went. Probably the majority of them knew
what priest was in each confessional; but I knew not, nor
did it matter at all to me. What
worried me now was how to

get safely in there, how to get through my confession with as little confusion as possible, and then how to get safely out again. I saw that I must kneel in the train of those who were to be confessed, one after the other, and follow them as they drew nearer and nearer to the curtain that hung before the little closets of the confessional; and so, finally, there would be nothing for me to do but to enter as the last one made his exit. I did this, with my heart climbing up into my very throat as I got closer and closer to the closeted priest. I was intent upon my prayers, and upon the formula with which I had striven to make myself familiar, and was almost unconsciously getting on and on toward the hidden one. All at once some one who was next before me arose and disappeared; I looked after him; he had secreted himself behind the swaying curtain.

There was a pause, a very long pause it seemed to me, and then I heard a rustling and a clatter as of a sliding shutter. A penitent emerged from the farther side of the confessional, and his place was immediately filled by another.

By this time I heard unintelligible whispering near me, or a deep sigh now and again, and soothing sibilants that flowed continually, until the invisible shutter was slid back again. Almost immediately my side of the confessional was vacated. I arose and entered, kneeling fearfully in that small chamber— no doubt one of the smallest chambers in all the world. A heavy green curtain shut in the darkness; I saw only that there was a crucifix upon one hand, and a little square lattice, with a gauze screen behind it, directly in front of me; and that this lattice was closed by a solid inner shutter. I heard faintly the whisper of the confessor, who was beyond the screen; and I waited now full of contentment and quite at ease.

The exquisite sense of secrecy and security — as if I were literally out of the world, and far beyond its reach—thrilled me with a strange joy. It seemed to me that there I could wait for hours without impatience; but I heard the rustle and the clatter again, and in the next moment the inner shutter was slid away, and I saw the profile of a priest (whom I had frequently seen) dimly outlined against the faint gray light that shone beyond him. It was a sudden though not unexpected climax, and I was thrown off my guard. I began in great embarrassment the confession which I had made to myself over and over again, and in less than half a moment found myself hopelessly involved. There was but one thing to be done then, and I did it with

all my heart; I threw myself
upon the mercy of my confessor.
I said: "Father, this is my first
confession; please help me to
make a good one." From that
moment I felt as if I held God's
ambassador by the hand—and
how I clung to him! I felt as
if he had thrown his protecting
arm about me; as if he would
henceforth 'aid me and encour-
age me and sustain me, and
stand between me and the
temptations of the world. I
then had but one wish: it was
that I might search my heart,
and find if in some dark corner
of it there were not still the
shadow of a lurking sin, and
that I might then root it out
and bring it to him in absolute
contrition. I wanted him not
to dismiss me yet, but to
reprove me again as gently
and as gravely as at first, and
to offer me once more the consolation he had already so freely
given. Then came the absolu-

tion, like a fountain of healing
and refreshment; and I was
bidden to go in peace.

O what joy entered into my
soul when I passed from that
confessional and prostrated myself before the altar of the
Mother of God! Rapt in the
profound spirit of love and trust
and gratitude, I felt the inex-
pressible happiness of the child
who knows that he is freely
and wholly forgiven.

. . . . . .

Long after I was in Rome.
There was a *fête* at the American
College, and a priest from my
old home, with whom I had
passed many hours among the
shrines of the Holy City—one
whose singular privilege it was
to decline a bishopric,—was
entertaining some of the not-
able foreign prelates who were
present with reminiscences of
our far country. Again and
again he had appealed to me
to bear him witness when the

Monseigneurs expressed amazement at the prolific spawn of American infidelity.

"He knows," said my reverend friend; "for he is a convert, and has been familiar with unbelievers."

"Yes, Father," cried I; "and it was to you that I made my first confession!"

He had not known it till that hour.

XX.

The supreme moment was near: on the morrow, at early Mass, I was to make my First Communion. No one knew of this, save Father A—— and my godfather; and they alone knew of my private baptism. It was a solemn night for me which preceded this crowning joy. I slept little, and then but lightly; more than once in my feverish dreams I approached the altar, and as the celebrant exposed the consecrated Host a chime of silver bells clashed in my ears, and I suddenly awoke, feeling myself unworthy to receive the Body of Our Lord. How thirsty I grew with a double thirst—the thirst of the lips and the thirst of the heart! And the thirst of my lips seemed to me to be

a temptation sent by the evil
one to confound me in the last
hour.

In the gray light of the morning I stole noiselessly out of
the house and hastened to the
cathedral. The great sanctuary
was already filled with the
multitude of the faithful, who
were humbling themselves in the
presence of the Divine One. I
felt myself the humblest and the
least worthy of them all, as I
made again and again the acts
of faith, contrition, and divine
love. I hid myself away, absorbed in devotion, and a priest
soon entered to begin the Mass.
With what reverence I followed
it! yet thinking always upon
the moment when I should be
summoned to the altar to
receive from those hands the
Bread of Eternal Life. A bell
tinkled; my heart leaped within
me; the next moment I was
filled with intense emotion; I
saw the linen spread upon the

altar railing, and the commu-
nicants clustering there. No
sooner had one retired than
another filled his place; and
presently I found myself — I
know not how — kneeling there,
and the priest approaching,
with the ciborium borne before
him.

I could not take my eyes from
the sacred Victim; I felt the
tears gathering; I heard the
voice of him who was about
to offer me the divine particle
quivering as he said, "*Corpus
Domini nostri Jesu Christi cus-
todiat animam tuam in vitam
æternam.*" A delicious perfume
seemed to distil upon my lips,
where was deposited, with inex-
pressible tenderness, the Blessed
Sacrament. Invisible choirs
chanted, "Holy, holy, holy!"
and the love which casteth out
all fear filled me to overflowing
with unspeakable peace.

. . . .

Alone in my chamber at home,

all that day I wondered if I
could ever again stain my lips
with even a careless word; wondered how this mighty privilege
can be neglected or abused by
those whose birthright it is;
wondered what there could be
to long for or to live for or
to hope for beyond the pale of
the one true Church, into whose
majestical bosom I had been
received!

XXI.

Now came the day of tribula-
tion, when I was tried as by
fire. Upon the first favorable
occasion, I told my people, one
and all, that I had been baptized
a Catholic. Though they were
certainly not surprised, and
were, perhaps, not greatly
grieved, they were, doubtless,
somewhat disappointed; and
from that day to this—now
many years—not one of them
has ever attended a religious
service with me. Never has the
least unkind or uncharitable
word been uttered in my
presence; on the contrary, they
have shown the sweetest toler-
ance at all times; have served
fish on Fridays without fail,
and have asked me to notify
them of the approach of other
fast-days or days of abstinence.

Among my friends, even among my intimate friends, and especially in the case of two or three frequent guests of the house, it was otherwise. The fact of my conversion was soon made public; a personal item to that effect went the rounds of the local journals and ultimately found its way into the Protestant religious press. Whatever may have been said to my parents by their more bigoted co-religionists I know not, for all that was likely to wound my feelings was kept discreetly from me; but I saw in more ways than one that I was no longer held in the same esteem by my associates, and some of them took pains to insult or ridicule me whenever they found opportunity. A few satisfied themselves with merely passing me on the street without recognition, or ignoring my presence when we met in society.

On one occasion a company of
my schoolmates, with whom
I had previously been on the
best of terms, locked the door of
the room in which we were
assembled to pass a social
evening, and there they amused
themselves for an hour or more
by ridiculing the ceremonials, of
whose sacred significance they
were ignorant; even of the forms
themselves they knew nothing
beyond the glimpses they had
caught during brief, occasional
loungings at a chapel door
during service. They burlesqued
the Litany, and descended to
blasphemous pantomimic imi-
tations of the ceremonials of the
Mass. I was held in my chair
by two powerful youths during
this disgraceful orgy, and not
suffered to depart until the par-
ticipants had grown weary of
their own sacrilege. Let me add,
to the credit of these young men,
that nearly all of them afterward made me an apology,

though they had no excuse to
offer for their misconduct.

Often I was bluntly assured
that I had made a fool of myself,
and that in less than a year I
should bitterly repent the step
I had taken. To these assaults
I invariably made no reply; I
dared not. I felt that I could
offer my friends no proof of my
wisdom and honesty in taking
the step I had taken,—no proof
so convincing as to show them
by my after-life that I had made
no mistake; that, in fact, I had
done only what I ought to have
done, and in doing it had left
nothing undone. I could not
always blame them for their
injustice to me; if, in my earlier
years, any one had assured me
that I would eventually become
a Catholic, I should, no doubt,
have been more indignant than
I was at the obloquy now
heaped upon me.

One man, an old friend of the
family, who often filled a seat

at our table, met me in the
street shortly after my conversion. I saw his face flush
furiously as we drew near to
each other, and the moment
he was about to pass me he
stopped short, shook his fist in
my face, and hissed, "You'll
shortly regret this, my fine
young fellow!" Even one of my
most intimate and best loved
friends—a man very much my
elder, and to whom I was like
a foster-child—said to me one
day: "I must confess to you
that you have fallen greatly in
my esteem."

Thus I was gradually cut off
from my old associations, and
a high wall seemed to be hedg-
ing me about. The sudden
anger of my friends and associates eventually began to cool;
amicable relations were slowly
resumed, though the subject of
my conversion was always a
forbidden one. But those friends
were never the same friends to

me, nor can they ever be. I had lost something in the estrangement—I hardly knew what,—and it was a sore loss to me at the time; but for that loss I had gained a thousandfold. I had learned the mutability of all human friendship, and learned it when I was most in need of the sympathy of those whom I had loved and trusted.

New sorrows lay in wait for me. My father met with serious reverses; the family circle was broken up and scattered hither and yon; almost immediately upon this trial followed the sudden death of two well-beloved brothers. I was left alone in my modest lodgings, struggling to obtain a livelihood. Bereaved, betrayed, disheartened, my spirit fainted within me, and my health began to fail. It was then that I found Holy Church to be my sole reliance.

XXII.

My confessor and chosen friend, a young priest of a cheerful temperament and possessed of great vitality, came often to my room; whenever he found himself in the vicinity of my lodgings, he would drop in for a few moments, and his presence was always invigorating and healthful.

Seeing that I needed a change of scene to reawaken my interest in life, he said to me one morning: "Can you conveniently give me two or three days of your time, and give them wholly to me without question, for me to do what I please with?" I answered that the days were alike to me, and that he was welcome to as many as he could make use of. "Then pack your portmanteau, and be

ready for me at seven o'clock
to-morrow morning. The carriage will be at the door."

I listlessly acquiesced. At
seven o'clock the carriage *was*
at the door, and within it I saw
the jovial face of my confessor,
my companion, who seemed a
very boy in the exuberant anticipation of his holiday. We drove
rapidly to the railway station,
and were whirled away through
the green dales of spring. At a
little village not too many miles
from town, we exchanged our
seats in the train for more lofty
ones on the box beside the driver
of an old-fashioned stage-coach.
There he made merry as we
toiled over the breezy hills and
bowled through the warm,
sweet-scented valleys, taking
our way toward the sea-coast,
where we arrived at evening.

It was a quiet house we
stopped at, one within sound of
the sea-surf; having good fishing
in the stream that brawled

beside the door, and good shoot-
ing among the hills that almost
overshadowed us. What long,
long talks we had there—we
two the only guests in the place,
and everybody leaving us quite
to our own diversions! What
long, long walks, and what
sport, also,—for my companion
was an expert angler and a
capital shot! Dreamy, restful
days were those we spent
together. While he read his
Office, pacing up and down the
veranda, I swung in the ham-
mock among the rose-trees and
envied him his vocation. When
our hour of rest came, we
wandered down by the sea, and,
throwing ourselves upon the
shining sand, just out of reach
of the waves, he told me
wonderful tales of his seminary
life in Rome, and of the almost
daily pilgrimages those colle-
gians of the Propaganda make
to the thousand-and-one shrines
of the Eternal City. "You must

go to Rome," said he; "you
must not rest night or day till
you have set out on your
journey; nor then even, nor ever
till you have knelt at the feet of
Christ's Vicar." Thus he began
to awaken me to life again.
Once more I enjoyed the sunshine and the sea, and the fresh
air of the morning; nor did he
pause until he won a smile from
me, as he laid before me his plan
for my foreign tour.

Many a time I had been told
that I had only to go into a
Catholic country to become at
once disgusted with the faith
and with the faithful; this was
oftenest the assurance of those
who had never been able to see
for themselves, but who relied
for their authority upon the
published works of anti-Catholic
travellers. Even those luke-
warm admirers of the Church
who are free to acknowledge the
picturesqueness of her external
appurtenances, imagined that

I should be shocked by the customs of the country as I drew near to the fountain-head óf the faith. My confessor, the story of whose Roman life I had learned by heart; who had filled me with the traditions of his college and of the Propaganda; who had made the way plain for me, so that already I began to feel at home in my dreams of Old-World travel,—he did not fear to urge me at once into the fields of the faith. Nor did he rest till he had bidden me God-speed as I set out on my pilgrimage—a pilgrimage that was not only to make me familiar with the Basilica of St. Peter and the palace of his successor, but was destined to carry my weary feet along the *Via Dolorosa*, as, with uncovered head, I entered the gates of Jerusalem on my way to Calvary and the Holy Sepulchre.

XXIII.

No sooner had I commenced my pilgrimage than I received unmistakable and indisputable assurances of the unity and universality of the Church of God. When I entered the primitive chapels in the Irish wilderness, and knelt among the impoverished peasantry, it was a familiar voice that spoke to us from the altar. I heard it again in that small convent far away on the shore of the Nile. The deep and unbroken silence of the desert was over us like a spell; the plash of the mighty waters, mingling with an occasional cry of our boatmen, or the sharp bark of some Nubian village dog, was all the sound that fell upon our ears for many days. In the midst of this profound stillness, while even in our waking hours we seemed to slumber, suddenly out of the breathless morning dropped the golden notes of a bell! The blare of a trumpet could not have been more startling, and with one accord we sprang to our feet and listened.

There are no bells in the Orient. Five times a day the *muezzin* cries, in a high, shrill voice, a call to prayer; and because the Mahometan is all-powerful there he does not choose to listen to the bells of the Christian Church. Here was the voice of one of them crying in the wilderness, and suffered to cry only because it was in the wilderness and far removed. We looked with eager eyes, and just before us, upon the long, low shore of the myste-rious river, we saw a convent wall. We sailed up under the shadow of the wall, and were made welcome by a grave Brother of St. Francis. In his charge we were shown over the quaint old building, its cloister fragrant with roses, and its cells so small and bare; and in an inner chamber, hidden away as in a fortress stood the holy altar, while before the Blessed Sacrament burned the unquenchable lamp.

That voice!—I heard it a thousand times repeated under the soaring dome of St. Peter's fane, and within sight of the seraglio of the Sultan at Stamboul; by the waters of the Greek Sea, and where the palms cluster along the reefs of the South Pacific, and the worshipers are the half-clad children of nature, who have scarcely yet awakened from their sleep of barbarism. It spoke to me in perpetual reassurance from the deck of a ship-of-the-line, when the French sailors stood with bowed heads and recited the *Angelus Domini*, as the sun went down into the blue, fathomless ocean.

Shall I ever forget that Easter in Jerusalem, when all the nations of the earth seemed to be gathered together under one banner and into one fold; when every color under heaven dyed the skins of the worshipers, and the costumes of the pilgrims were a pageant, and their speech the confusion of Babel? Yet the voice from the altar was intelligible to each and all of us; and the priests, who had come in from the four quarters of the globe, spoke in the common tongue, and could speak to one another only in the common tongue—the same which we heard from the altar.

As I journeyed, all the wayside shrines throughout the length and breadth of Europe; all the calvaries, with their agonies wrought in marble; all the crucifixes, and medallions, and pictures of saints and angels, with swinging lamps that twinkle nightly before

them; all the fountains where
the holy ones have slaked their
thirst, and in that act have
hallowed them forever; all the
caves where they have suffered
and the cells where they have
lived and died; all the inanimate
objects that have been sanctified
by touch or association, and
have become animate by
reason of this—all, all seemed
to me to be personal and
perpetual congratulations and
felicitations and benedictions
addressed to each of us. If my
faith was a blind faith before,
it was almost blinding now;
for I lived and moved and had
my being in the actual presence
of those amazing testimonials
of the unity and universality
of Holy Church.

XXIV.

At Rome I met with a serious accident. My horse stumbled with me in the Campagna, at the dead of night, and together we were precipitated from the edge of a low bridge into the dry bed of a creek. My escape from death was considered almost miraculous. My first thought was of the Church, the cherishing mother into whose lap I longed to throw myself, trusting all to her wisdom and her power. For many weeks I was confined to a bed of pain, but my heart was with her, and I knew that every day—for my case was known—there went up from her altars a prayer for my recovery. She was my hope in this extremity, and I was always looking forward to the hour

when I might once more enter
her sacred portals and pour out
my heart in love and gratitude
to her for my deliverance.

My first visit, on my recovery,
was to the Lateran Basilica; it
stands against the gate through
which I was borne on the sorry
night of my mishap. O melting
hour, that found me a cripple,
though convalescent, dissolved
in tears before the altar in the
mother of all churches!

All the bells of Rome were
music in my ears—the music
that beguiled me in my long
confinement; and when they
rang the *Ave Maria*, it seemed
to me that ten thousand glorious tongues were loosed to
syllable her praise. Never—no,
never—could I escape from
their salutations, for the church-
bells ring incessantly in those
dear lands. Many a time, in
the solemn silence of the
Venetian night, have I listened
for the clang of the brazen-

throated bell that proclaimed
the midnight hour; I knew then
that in the cool cloisters of San
Georgio Maggiore, over the
dark lagoon, the sandalled feet
of the monks were seeking the
oratory, where prayers are
nightly said; I knew that in a
little while the Holy Sacrifice of
the Mass would be offered upon
a myriad altars — the Sacrifice
that is perpetually offered; for it
is always morning somewhere.
I knew that the unceasing
prayer of the faithful would be
caught up, like an echo that
rolls round the world forever
and forever; and I folded my
hands in peace and fell asleep,
reposing, full of love and trust,
in the bosom of Holy Church.

Thus it was that the faith in
the land of the faithful affected
me. Seldom could I pass even
one of the many chapels (the
doors standing always invitingly open), without entering
and kneeling in that serene

atmosphere for at least a few moments. All care and worry and discontent stopped without the portals; those feared to enter there. What if I knew that I was to take up the burden again—or at least a part of it—when I passed out into the street? I knew that I could resort as often as I pleased to this saving sanctuary, for no one could prevent me; I knew that in that Catholic land, and in every land where the Altar of God is raised, the Church was my impregnable fortress and the strength of my deliverance!

XXV.

How much, how very much of our reliance is in the Fatherhood of the clergy—the clergy who in their divine office are the oracles of God! Where are you now, young priest, who first turned my feet out of the darkness into the light? Lost to me in the unity of the priesthood— you the merest fractional part of the whole;—but somewhere, if you still live, enlightening the ignorant, helping the needy, counselling the perplexed, giving your days to works of mercy and your nights to prayer.

And thou who wast my confessor, to whom my heart was as an open page, wherein thou mightest read to the last syllable—whither has duty called thee; for inclination thou hadst none, save to serve thy

Lord and Master? Admirable
Order of reverend and spiritual
Fathers! With what zeal I
sought the superior, who had
graciously summoned me from
the distractions of London to
the pastoral shades at Roe-
hampton! I could not have
been more at ease in the first
moment of our meeting had I
known this reverend Jesuit, and
been known of him, all my
days; and so we walked and
talked, and viewed the riches
and the beauties of the mother
house, till I was loath to leave
and be thrown back again upon
the world.

And thou unknown and un-
named confessor, whom I sought
in the unparalleled Cathedral of
Milan (within whose splendid
crypt are treasured the relics of
my patron Saint), didst thou
not take me to thy heart, out
of the hurly-burly, and tenderly
shrive me, and as tenderly keep
me by thee till thou hadst

offered the Holy Sacrifice upon
the sumptuous altar where San
Carlo's very body is enshrined?
—never again to see thee, or to
know thee; but thou art one
with all of these, our Fathers;
and my gratitude is thine
forever.

Illustrious Monseigneur who
unlocked the mysteries of Rome
for me, and made straight my
paths in the mazes of that maze-
ful city; in whose home I was
at home; at whose hospitable
board I was made welcome; who
led me to the feet of the Holy
Father; whose unremitting
kindness spared me many a
grief,—shall I ever again behold
you, and commune with you
in the flesh, in the old fashion
which has made Rome a blessed
memory to me.

Cowled and tonsured monk,
whose happiness it is to dwell
within the City of the Holy
Sepulchre; whom I sought upon
the eve of Easter, and from

whose hands I received His
Body upon the Mount where
He was crucified,—have I not
the tangible proof of our most
precious conference, the treasured document thou gavest me,
and which runs as follows:

[Seal.]

In Dei Nomine. Amen.

Omnibus, et singulis præsentes literas
inspecturis, lecturis, vel legi audituris,
fidem, notumque facimus, Nos Terræ .
Sanctæ Custos, Devotum Peregrinum
[name] Jerusalem feliciter pervenisse die
12 Aprilis, anni 1876: inde subsequen-
tibus diebus præcipua sanctuaria, in
quibus mundi Salvator dilectum popu-
lum suum, imo et totius humani
generis perditam congeriem ab inferi ser-
vitute misericorditer liberavit, utpote
Calvarium ubi cruci affixus, devicta
morte, cœli januas nobis aperuit; SS.
Sepulcrum, ubi sacrosanctum ejus Corpus reconditum, triduo ante suam
gloriosissimam Resurrectionem quievit;
ac tandem ea omnia Sacra Palestinæ
Loca gressibus Domini, ac Beatissimæ
ejus Matris Mariæ consecrata, a religiosis
nostris et Peregrinis visitari solita,
visitasse, Sanctam Missam audivisse
necnon Sacramenta Pœnitentiæ et Eu-
charistiæ frequentasse. In quorum fidem
has scripturas officii nostri sigillo

munitas per Secretarium expediri man-
davimus.

Datis Jerusalem, ex venerabili nostro
Conventu SS. Salvatoris, die [date].

FR. BARNABASSAB TUTERAMNA.

[Seal.]   Secretarius Terræ Sanctæ.

But it is all the same, or
should be all the same, whoever
or wherever they may be —
whether in the bogs of the
Green Isle or in the Celestial
City. The Fatherhood is above
us and about us, and stands
between us and the world, from
the metropolis to the antipodes.

How often have I fled to
some reverend Father for relief;
to some poor priest, perhaps,
whose meagre fare was of fish
and cocoanuts; whose house
was thatched with palm leaves;
whose labors, corporeal as well
as spiritual, were far beyond
his strength! He has shared
his crumb with me, and by his
cheerful example and manly
encouragement has given me
new life, in the hope of making myself worthy to be the

spiritual son of such a father.
Many a time has the priest of
some provincial parish set out
his cup of thin wine, his crust
of bread, and his lump of goat's-
milk cheese—all that he had to
offer; and it was offered with
a show of genuine and loving
hospitality that made each
morsel sweeter to the lips than
honey. Even when we have
been unable to speak any common tongue there was a bond
of sympathy, a responsive echo
in our hearts—a brave, strong
sentiment, filial and fraternal,
peculiar to the Catholic Church,
and utterly impossible in any
other faith whatever.

Shade of our most Holy
Father Pio Nono, whose powerful intercession I now humbly
crave! it was at thy feet I
knelt twice and thrice, thy
mellifluous voice I heard, thy
hand that was laid upon my
brow, and thy pen that signed
my plenary indulgence. Thy

blessing has consecrated the precious crucifix now hanging by my bedside, and this statue of thy great predecessor, whose chair thou didst gloriously fill so many years; these beads and medals passed from thy hand to me, sweet saint,—thou that wast the father of the Fathers who father us! Once Bishop of Rome, head of the Church Militant, Vicar of Christ on earth— now in the glory of the Church Triumphant,—may the efficacy of the grace thou didst impart to me abide with me forever!

XXVI.

What shall I say of the strong, beautiful, and noble sentiment which prevails throughout the Church, and which is not to be found in any human institution, however loudly it may boast the spirit that is supposed to inspire it,—I refer to the brotherhood of the faithful! Take the whole catalogue of organizations and societies, whether religious or charitable or social or political —secret or open,—and where among them will you find the same temper and disposition as among the faithful? where the same ardor, enthusiasm, earnestness, courage, and unanimity? where the same liberty in the enjoyment of the supreme privileges of the sanctuary—fraternity in the common bond of love and trust, and uncompromising equality in the rights of each individual member of the Church? The prince and the pauper kneel shoulder to shoulder before the altar, and unburden their souls at the feet of the selfsame shriver. It does not disturb me if I find upon my right hand the African, were he ever so black; on my left the swarthy Coolie; before me the beggar who knocks daily at my door to ask for food; and behind me the president of a college, the actress from a minor theatre, or the first artist or lawyer in the land. In all probability, they are unconscious of my presence, as I usually am, and always should be, of theirs. In every case we have sunk our individuality and have become one, by reason of a common love, a common hope, a common trust in the saving grace of the holy Sacraments.

How often have I been touched at the respect paid the dead in Catholic countries;

at the reverence with which the
business man, hastening to ful-
fil the duties of the hour, pauses
and lifts his hat as the funeral
of the unknown passes him in
the street! What pity streams
from the eyes of the poor
woman who kneels in her
humble doorway, and, crossing
herself, prays for the repose
of the soul that was never
known to her in this life; but
the body is borne toward the
cemetery, and she joins her
prayer to the many that are
freely offered along the solemn
way!

How often have I joined the
sad procession that grew and
grew as we trod the rough pavement of some little Italian
town, following the good priest
who was bearing the Holy
Viaticum to the house of
affliction! The bell was ringing
in advance of him and the tapers
flaring in the wind; and before
teh door o that house we knelt,

uncovered, in the rain or the shine, repeating the while, in our several languages, the Recommendation of a Departing Soul. "Pray for me! pray for me!" He was a stranger who asked it, but he was a Catholic and in great physical anguish, and one and all prayed fervently, then and there, for his speedy recovery or happy death.

In the public eating-houses, the wine-shops, and the suburban summer-gardens, where the Italians and the Spanish congregate for pleasure and recreation, lamps burn always before the shrine of the loved Madonna, and the felicitations on holydays are hearty and unanimous. The joyous congratulations at Easter, the universal sorrow in Lent, especially the profound grief of the community when it passes bodily in an involuntary pilgrimage from chapel to chapel, to dwell for a moment

upon the agony of our crucified
Redeemer, and to mourn over
the tomb where they have laid
Him,—this is entirely Catholic
and peculiarly Roman. Remind
me not, O Brothers in the faith!
remind me not of that dear
past when, by your side, I made
the daily round of the Lenten
Stations in the Eternal City.
Oh, the delight of those Roman
days, though lost to us, forgotten never more. The almost
childish delight of the people
over the dainty cribs at Christ-
mas, and the innocent hilarity
of   Epiphany,—these   and   a
thousand others are sentiments
shared in common by the whole
body of Holy Church, and prove
beyond peradventure the excep-
tional, the almost phenomenal
genuineness of the brotherhood
of the faithful.

XXVII.

How could the faithful fail
to be more than tolerant, even
more than neighborly, one
toward another, when the Holy
Sacrifice of the Mass is daily
offered for the common good
of all? "To me nothing is so
consoling, so piercing, so thrilling, so overcoming, as the
Sacrifice of the Mass, said as
it is among us,"— so wrote
the great and good Cardinal
Newman. He adds: "I could
attend Masses forever and not
be tired. It is not a mere form
of words: it is a great action—
the greatest action that can be
on earth. It is not the invoca-
tion merely, but, if I dare use
the word, the evocation of the
Eternal." It is the Sacred
Drama daily, hourly, perpetually enacted upon the altars

of the whole world; the Passion, Agony and Death, vicariously suffered for our sakes,—a divine tragedy of singular simplicity, of unparalleled pathos, in the witnessing of which hard, indeed, is the heart that is not melted!

When I recall my first impressions of the Mass—if in my bewilderment I can be said to have received any impression whatever,—I assure myself that the majority of Protestants and unbelievers, who look coldly or curiously upon the altar, are as little mindful of the sacred significance of the Sacrifice and as unworthy spectators as I was. Oh, the loss to these! Do we not see in the gravity of the celebrant as he bears the chalice to the altar, Our Lord entering the Garden of Gethsemane? It is the first scene in the mystical drama, and every breath is hushed. The divine One is burdened with a foreknowledge of

His doom. He kneels in the garden: the Holy Sacrifice begins; we kneel with Him, and are to follow Him, step by step, to the very end.

At the *Confiteor* He has fallen upon His face, bathed in the sweat of blood; He is betrayed with a kiss, led away captive, grievously smitten, and denied. The celebrant turns to us at the *Dominus vobiscum*, and in his glance we see the conversion of Peter. Our Lord is led before Pilate, brought to Herod, scornfully sent back again to Pilate. He is spoiled of His garments— at the unveiling of the chalice,— scourged and crowned with thorns. Pilate washes his hands of the crime, and at the moment the celebrant moistens his fingers. "Behold the Man!" cries Pilate; and the voice from the altar pleads, "*Orate fratres.*"

At the Preface we hear the warning bell. The awful progress of the tragedy is watched

in breathless silence; only from
the organ-loft comes the wail
of the singers. The bell rings:
He is condemned to death, and
made to bear His cross, while
His brow is wiped with the
handkerchief of Veronica, and
the effigy of that sorrowful
Face is retained forever. He is
nailed to the cross, and at the
Elevation of the Host, while
the chiming bells mark every
posture of the celebrant at the
altar; while the torch-bearers
gather about, the smoking
censers are swung aloft, the
flowers are scattered upon the
air, and, if it be a Military
Mass, the whole body silently
presents arms; while the devout
kneelers bow their heads and
beat their breasts in contrition,
lo! the cross is raised on high.
A moment later the elevated
chalice seems to catch the water
and the blood that gush from
the riven Heart of Him who
died for us.

In the *Memento*, which follows, He is praying for the world; He is merciful to the penitent thief; He thirsts, and He utters the Seven Words upon the cross. (Here the *Pater Noster* is loudly chanted.) He dies, He descends into hell; and at the *Agnus Dei*, while the bells chime again, there is the conversion of many at the cross. In Holy Communion we commemorate His burial, and His anointing in the last ablution of the celebrant. His Resurrection follows, and He appears to His disciples at the *Dominus vobiscum*. The last Collect is a memory of His forty days with the disciples; the last *Dominus vobiscum*, of His glorious ascension; and with the Benediction descends the Holy Ghost!

O marvellous Sacrament! mysterious, majestical! O never-failing source of joy! what a privation is theirs who, having

once known Thee, are parte
from Thee! How do they sur-
vive who trust not in Thee,
who hope not through Thee,
and who seek Thee and know
Thee not?

XXVIII.

Holy Virgin, our Blessed Lady, who hast graciously appeared to us, and who hast appeared only unto us! Mother of God, and of Christ, who is God; Mother of divine grace; most pure, most chaste, undefiled, inviolate; most amiable, most admirable; Mother of our Creator and of our Redeemer! how can we forget thee, remembering what thou wast and art and ever shalt be!

Blessed day that found me threading the narrow streets of Bethlehem, kneeling at the shrine of the Nativity, glorious with the light that shone from clusters of golden lamps, and the Golden Star in the midst thereof—the star that is adored to-day by the true Magi of the earth! Day most blessed that

found me mourning with thee
upon Calvary, and beside the
stone of the sepulchre, and de-
scending reverently into the
grotto of thy tomb! Blessed
evening at the close of that
blessed day in Loreto, when
the thousands and tens of
thousands of pilgrims had gone
to their weary beds upon the
pavements or among the neighboring pastures and vineyards,
even there to hymn thy praises
to the stars, thou Star of stars!
—when the young monk led me
by a private door into that
great temple, and alone we
entered the Holy House that
was borne by angels away from
the desecrations of the bar-
barous infidel, and at last set
upon the hill whose name has
become glorious throughout
the earth! Blessed beads and
medals that have been pressed
against the stones of the Holy
House, and laid within the
precious bowls that thou didst

use in Nazareth, and that were
deposited upon the altar within
the Holy House where thy
sacred and supernatural image
stands, and were blessed again,
to mind me of my privielges,
then and there! Blessed Rock
of Lourdes, within whose cleft
she stood, and spoke articulate
words, while at her feet the very
breast of nature was stirred, so
that a fountain gushed forth as
from the heart of it, and is
to-day confounding the wise
and making wise the foolish!
Blessed souvenir, thou wee
statuette of silver, in case of
bluest velvet, that hast been
dipped in that fount of grace,
the miraculous flood of Lourdes,
and goest with me where I go,
a talisman most precious!

O Virgin most prudent, most
renowned, most powerful, merciful and faithful! whose sorrows
have wrung my heart, whose
joys have thrilled me; before
whose mirrored graces, as set

forth in marble or upon canvas, I have cast myself in my extremity, and lit my votive taper, and anointed myself with the oil of the sacred lamps. Mirror of justice, Seat of wisdom, Cause of our joy: if but they all might know thee as we know thee and love thee as we love thee! Spiritual vessel, Vessel of honor, Vessel of singular devotion: touch their hearts. Mystical rose, whose fragrance intoxicates the soul; Tower of David, Tower of ivory, House of gold: shine upon them and fill their eyes with light. Ark of the Covenant, Gate of heaven: may they be made worthy to enter in to thee! Morning Star, illumine their everlasting night; Health of the weak, restore them to the bosom of that fold without which there is no strength; Refuge of sinners, oh! receive them; Comforter of the afflicted, gather them in thine arms and comfort them. Help of Christians, aid us so to live that we may enlighten them by our example. Queen of angels and of patriarchs and prophets; Queen of Apostles and of martyrs and confessors; Queen of virgins and of all saints; Queen of Heaven, pray for us!

XXIX.

Picture the barrenness of a mind that can not conceive the idea of a saint; of a heart that refuses to accept the amazing proofs of human perfection achieved through the aid of special grace, absolute humility, and the purifying, sanctifying, consuming love of God! No Protestant, no infidel can do this; he is, therefore, cut off from the fellowship which the Catholic is permitted to share with the saints in glory.

With a single exception, the saints were, like us, conceived in sin. Three nativities alone does the Church commemorate — Our Lord's, our Blessed Lady's, and St. John's; but what a crowd of witnesses assemble at the Throne of Grace! Consider the extraor-

dinary company of holy angels
and archangels; of all the holy
orders of blessed spirits; of
patriarchs and prophets; of
Apostles, Evangelists, and disciples of our Lord. Consider the
Holy Innocents and martyrs;
the bishops, confessors, doctors,
priests and levites; the monks
and hermits, the virgins and
widows, and all the holy men
and women saints of God, on
whom we are permitted to call
in prayer. Their supernatural
virtues are proved by their supernatural acts; their miracles bear
them witness a thousandfold.

Miracles! Not in one of all
their miracles do they defy the
laws of nature; but rather,
there is some subtle and superior
law of nature subservient to
them, and to them alone. The
miracle of yesterday or of to-
day or of the forever—the blind
receiving sight, the dumb speak-
ing, the lame and the halt walk-
ing, and even the dead brought

back to life, are disputed; yet the incontrovertible testimony of the multitudes of eye-witnesses stands to the truth of each and all of these. Miracles! These are our inheritance, and nowhere else is the like seen or heard of or dreamt of; and these are the scorn of the unbelieving, and by them are they received with measureless, impotent derision. What can they expect who hope nothing, trust nothing, believe nothing? On the steps of the precious altar in Naples, under my very eyes, within reach of my very hands and lips, the congealed blood of St. Januarius returned to life, and bubbled and throbbed within the vial which was twice enclosed within the reliquary, lightly poised in the hands of the Cardinal. "A mere chemical trick!" cry alike the scientist and the simpleton; "a trick which we can duplicate at pleasure." But they have

never duplicated it! Nor do
the boasts of the rationalists
avail aught. Still are the
shrines of the saints ablaze with
the glitter of ex-votos; the ban-
dit's dagger is laid at the feet
of the Madonna; the carbine
of the brigand is surrendered
before the altar of Our Lady,
and he returns into the wilderness with a heart as soft as
the lamb's fleece that covers his
broad shoulders, but with a
step as proud and manly as
ever trod the earth.

O beautiful ships! hewn with
deft and loving fingers in the
mariner's painful leisure, memo-
rials of his vow when delivered
out of the jaws of death, and
offered to thee, Notre Dame de
la Garde. Thy golden statue
crowns the dome of thy temple
upon the hilltop above Mar-
seilles; like a glimmering star
thou shinest upon the watery
track of the departing voyager;
and thou sendest afar the first

ray that welcomes him on his
return.

O touching and pathetic testimonials of grace received, indisputable, unanswerable proofs of
thy miraculous love, Our Lady
of Lourdes! There is the treas-
ury: the innumerable crutches,
rests, stretchers, strange wheel-
ing-chairs, and all the harnesses
of torture from which thou didst
deliver those suffering ones who
put their faith in thee, Our Lady
of Lourdes!

O saints'-days and name-days,
the birthdays of the soul! how
welcome your return — thrice
welcome, for the treble joy and
peace and love that are one with
you! O saints of God! tempted
in your turn, alike as we are,
but putting temptation far from
you, and dwelling alone with
God: you teach us by your
example what we may strive
to do; you prove to us by your
victory that to strive in your
spirit is to triumph in your

path. The knowledge of your weakness is our strength, and your strength our shield and buckler. How can any one refuse to know you, and, knowing you, refuse to love and reverence you! Even in death you are all-powerful, and live again in the very garments that clothed you in life, filling them with virtues potential. O everlasting examples of the infinite beauty of holiness, of the unconquerable power of love, and of the unfading lustre of charity and humility and innocence! We are yours, ye chosen of God, and would be one with you! O intercede for us!

XXX.

Alone no more forever! In the darkness of the night, in the solitude of the desert and of the sea, and in that more awful solitude which the stranger in a strange land knows and suffers, feeling himself the un-recognized decimal in the infinite multitude,—thou art with me, my ever-watchful and protecting Guardian Angel! I know not thy name nor the fashion of thy form or features; but in my dreams, waking or sleeping, I seem to see thee, clad in robes of beauty, thy wings folded in perfect peace, thy shining brow half shaded by locks celestial, and thy calm eyes, that never close in slumber, fixed on mine with a glance of love unspeak-able. Often I must grieve thee, for I am human and thou art

divine; but because thou art
divine thou wilt pity and for-
give my human weakness. How
can I sin in thy sight, immacu-
late spirit! How can I yield to
the temptations of the seducer!
With what anguish must thou
follow my wilful. and stumbling
steps, throwing thine arms
about me in the moment of
my fall; seeking, alas! vainly,
to lead me back into the
straight way; pricking my con-
science with the thorn of re-
proof, till it cries out against
me in thy name and with thy
voice!

Silent counsellor! how often
hast thou stood between me
and the unseen or unheeded
danger that was threatening
me! How tenderly hast thou
smoothed the pillow on my
bed of pain, and witnessed with
grief the torments of this poor
body! In my saddest hour, perchance, thou hast mingled thy
tears with mine, and folded me

to thy heart to compassionate me—and I not mindful of thee! Heavenly guest, whose home is in my heart I give thee a thousand times ten thousand welcomes! Let me not lose thee, nor forget thee, nor cease from reposing trustfully in thee, O loving and beloved! In my last hour may thy arms receive my fainting soul, and thy bosom sustain it in its agony!

XXXI.

I do not know what hope the
Protestant has in the future of
the departed soul. As for the
infidel, he has none whatever,
and this is his pitiful boast.
The Protestant believer launches
the spirit into space; from that
melancholy moment it is no
more to him than a memory—
a memory which, in the course
of nature, must fade away. He
hopes to follow in due season,
and vaguely hopes to find his
own somewhere among the
innumerable hosts of the im-
mortals; but until that hour
has come there is an absolute
separation, a complete sundering of all the natural ties of
affinity and consanguinity. The
separation is as absolute, the
sundering as complete, as if a
fathomless pit yawned between

them—a pit whose awful depths
echo no voice of hope, and from
whose distant limits shines no
familiar or unfamiliar form.
Their fellowship ends with the
grave. Can anything be sadder
than this? Of course, no reasonable being, within whose soul
has sprung one aspiration,
however feeble, can for a moment tolerate the theory of total
annihilation.

There are Protestants who
believe that "hell is paved with
infant skulls not a span long."
There are some who believe in
universal salvation; how could
heaven be more desirable than
earth in such a case? But the
majority of Protestants are
quite unsettled as to exactly
what they believe and what
disbelieve. How miserable must
be this state of uncertainty;
how cheerless the thought of a
future life; how bitter the pang
of death! Suffered to die help-
lessly, without the aid of the

sacraments, and dismissed into
the mysterious chamber beyond
the veil, alone, unguided and
unaided; its heavenly guardian
unheeded in death as in life;
the communion of the saints
unrecognized; the glory and the
majesty and the might of that
love which streams from the
Sacred Heart of Jesus and of
Mary most clement, Mother
of our Redeemer, denied and
derided:—what has not the
Protestant soul to unlearn, and
what to learn after that, before
it can enjoy the repose of the
faithful!

O Death! where is thy sting?
O Grave! where is thy victory,
when by the side of the bed of
death stands the one into whose
hands is given the power to
loose and to bind sin? Contrast
the death of the Protestant with
the death of the good Catholic.
I have already pictured the
former, and now it is the latter
that we look on, while the

prayers for the sick are said,
and the last Sacraments are
solemnly administered; while
the dying eyes are fixed upon
the image of our crucified
Redeemer and of Our Lady
of Sorrows; while the blessed
candle is in readiness, and the
blessed water is sprinkled from
time to time over and about the
devoted pillow; while perpetual
aspirations hover upon the lips,
and the "Last Sighs of the
Dying" are breathed into the
ear; while each throb of the
heart responds to the thrice
blessed names of Jesus, Mary,
and Joseph: when the "Recommendation of a Departing Soul"
—that glorious prayer, upon
the wings of which it is borne
heavenward—is recited:

"Receive Thy servant, O Lord!
into the place of salvation,
which he hopes from Thy mercy.
Amen.

"Deliver, O Lord! the soul of
Thy servant from all danger of

hell, from all pain and tribu-
lation. Amen.

"Deliver, O Lord! the soul of
Thy servant, as Thou didst
deliver Enoch and Elias from the
common death of the world.
Amen.

"As thou didst deliver Noe
from the flood; Abraham from
the midst of the Chaldeans; Job
from all his afflictions; Isaac
from sacrifice; Lot from the
flames of Sodom; Moses from
the hands of Pharaoh; Daniel
from the lions' den; the three
children from the fiery furnace,
and from the hands of an un-
merciful king; Susanna from
her false accusers; David from
the hands of Goliath and Saul;
and as Thou didst deliver that
blessed virgin 'and martyr, St.
Thecla, from most cruel torments, so vouchsafe to deliver
the soul of this Thy servant, and
bring it to the participation of
Thy heavenly joys. Amen."

So passes the faithful soul to

judgment; after which, if not ushered at once into the ineffable glory of the Father, it pauses for a season in the perpetual twilight of that border-land where the spirit is purged of the very memory of sin. Even as Our Lord Himself descended into Limbo; as He died for us, but rose again from the dead and ascended into heaven, so we hope to rise and follow Him, —sustained by the unceasing prayers of the Church, the intercession of the saints, and all the choirs of the just, who are called on night and day; and also by the prayers and pleadings of those who have loved us and who are still in the land of the living.

The prayers that ease the pangs of purgatory, the *Requiem*, the *Miserere*, the *De profundis* — these are the golden stairs upon which the soul of the redeemed ascends into everlasting joy. Even the Protestant

Laureate of England has confessed the poetical justice and
truth of this, and into the mouth
of the dying Arthur — that
worthy knight — he puts these
words:

> Pray for my soul! More things are
>   wrought by prayer
> Than this world dreams of; wherefore
>   let thy voice
> Rise like a fountain for me night and
>   day:
> For what are men better than sheep or
>   goats
> That nourish a blind life within the
>   brain,
> If, knowing God, they lift not hands of
>   prayer
> Both for themselves and those who call
>   them friend?
> For so the whole round earth is every
>   way
> Bound by gold chains about the feet of
>   God.

O ye gentle spirits that have
gone before me, and that are
now, I trust, dwelling in the
gardens of Paradise, beside the
river of life that flows through
the midst thereof, — ye whose
names I name at the Memorial
for the Dead in the Holy Sac-

rifice of the Mass,—as ye look upon the lovely and shining countenances of the elect, and perchance upon the beauty of our Heavenly Queen, and upon her Son in glory,—O remember me who am still this side of the valley of the shadow, and in the midst of trials and tribulations. And you who have read these pages, written from the heart, after much sorrow and long suffering, though I be still with you in the flesh, or this poor body be gathered to its long home,—you whose eyes are now fixed upon this line, I beseech you

PRAY FOR ME!